VOLUME II

**by Debbie Dadey
and Marcia Thornton Jones**

illustrated by John Steven Gurney

SCHOLASTIC INC.

New York Toronto London Auckland Sydney
Mexico City New Delhi Hong Kong Buenos Aires

Frankenstein Doesn't Plant Petunias, ISBN 0-590-47071-X, Text copyright © 1993 by Marcia Thornton Jones and Debra S. Dadey. Illustrations copyright © 1993 by Scholastic Inc.

Aliens Don't Wear Braces, ISBN 0-590-47070-1, Text copyright © 1993 by Debbie Dadey and Marcia Thornton Jones. Illustrations copyright © 1993 by Scholastic Inc. Book design by Laurie McBarnette

Genies Don't Ride Bicycles, ISBN 0-590-47297-6, Text copyright © 1993 by Marcia Thornton Jones and Debbie Dadey. Book design by Laurie McBarnette

Pirates Don't Wear Pink Sunglasses, ISBN 0-590-47298-4, Text copyright © 1994 by Marcia Thornton Jones and Debbie S. Dadey. Book design by Laurie McBarnette

THE ADVENTURES OF THE BAILEY SCHOOL KIDS is a registered trademark of Scholastic Inc. All rights reserved. Published by Scholastic Inc. SCHOLASTIC and associated logos are trademarks and/or registered trademarks of Scholastic Inc.

12 11 10 9 8 7 6 5 4 3 2 1   5 6 7 8 9 10/0

Printed in the U.S.A.   40

This edition created exclusively for Barnes & Noble, Inc.
2005 Barnes & Noble Books

ISBN 0-7607-6768-8

First compilation printing, February 2005

Frankenstein Doesn't Plant Petunias

1
Field Trip

Melody twisted her black pigtail and looked out the bus window at the cloudy sky. "I can't wait to get to the Shelley Museum."

Mrs. Jeepers' third-grade class from Bailey Elementary School was on a bus heading for the Shelley Museum of Science. It was the last field trip before summer vacation. Melody was sitting in the middle of the bus with her friends Liza, Eddie, and Howie.

Howie nodded. "This is the best field trip ever!"

Eddie made a face. "Other kids get to go to Water World, but we have to go to an old science museum."

"Science museums can be a lot of fun," Melody told her friends. "I went to one in Indianapolis that was incredible."

"It's incredible that they didn't keep you for an exhibit." Eddie giggled.

"If the Shelley Museum is doing experiments on smart alecks, you'd better watch out." Melody stuck out her tongue at Eddie.

The kids on the bus bounced up and

down as they went over an old bridge. "My mother told me that the museum was closed after an electrical storm damaged the building," Melody said. "This is the first time it's been open in fourteen years. It's supposed to have lots of new stuff, even a prehistoric exhibit."

"Maybe there's a bat exhibit and Mrs. Jeepers can visit her friends," Eddie joked.

"Shhh, she's looking this way," Melody whispered. The four kids smiled as Mrs. Jeepers looked back from the front seat. Her long fire-red hair was neatly pulled back by a green bow. Purple fingernails gently rubbed the emerald-green brooch on her polka-dotted dress.

When Mrs. Jeepers turned to speak to the bus driver, Eddie bragged, "I'm not afraid of Mrs. Jeepers. I don't care if she is Count Dracula's cousin."

Mrs. Jeepers was from Transylvania and seemed to have special powers, especially when she rubbed her brooch. Most of the kids in the third grade at Bailey Elementary thought she was a vampire.

"I hope we get there soon," Liza said in a small voice. "This bus is making me sick."

"Hold on!" Howie said. "I think I see the museum."

"All I see is dust." Eddie coughed as they turned onto a dirt road. Dust filled the bus as it bounced from one pothole to another.

The kids covered their noses until the bus lurched to a stop. When the dust settled, they looked out the grimy windows.

"Now I *know* Mrs. Jeepers is batty," Eddie said.

2
The Shelley Museum

Everyone filed off the bus and stared up at the old museum. It was four stories tall and stood on the top of a hill surrounded by towering oak trees. Shingles were missing from the roof, and broken shutters banged in the wind. The whole building needed a paint job.

"This place looks like it's ready to fall in a heap," Melody said.

"I guess they never got around to fixing it after it was struck by lightning," Howie said.

"Maybe lightning fried the owner's brains." Eddie laughed.

A distant rumble of thunder could be heard as dark clouds swirled above.

"All right, children." Mrs. Jeepers clapped her hands. "Let us begin our tour." As she led the class up the crumbling steps of the museum, the yellow school bus disappeared down the long dirt road.

"Do you still feel sick?" Melody asked Liza. "You look a little pale."

Liza pulled her jacket tight and shrugged. "There's something very strange about this place."

"Like what?" Howie asked.

"I've seen it before," she said.

"But you've never been here," Melody said.

"I haven't," Liza whispered. "That's why it bothers me."

"Boogers bother you." Eddie rolled his eyes. "Come on, we have to catch up."

Mrs. Jeepers and the rest of the class were gathered in front of a huge wooden door.

"Where's the doorbell?" Carey asked.

Mrs. Jeepers smiled an odd little half smile. "This is a very old building. We must use the door knocker." She lifted the heavy iron knocker and let it fall with a thud.

There was no answer.

The third-graders huddled by the door. "Maybe no one's home," Liza said.

"Nonsense." Mrs. Jeepers smiled. "They are expecting us."

"I hope they hurry," Carey said. "It's starting to rain, and the bus won't be back for hours."

Then the door slowly creaked open.

3
Dr. Victor and Frank

Lightning cracked across the sky as Mrs. Jeepers and the third-graders stared up at a towering giant of a man. His long legs stuck out of his brown ragged pants, and a wrinkled white shirt stretched across his massive chest. His square face was pale next to his coal-black hair, and across his cheek was a huge purple scar.

"He's got a gun," Howie whispered to his friends. He pointed to the man's pocket where the handle of a pistol peeped out. The third-graders took one step away from the hulk as he glared down at the group of kids.

Mrs. Jeepers stretched out her hand and smiled. "Hello, I am Mrs. Jeepers,

and this is my class from Bailey Elementary School. We are here to visit the museum."

The giant lifted one enormous hand and pushed the door back. An ugly scar reached all around his bony wrist.

"Hrrmm," he grunted as Mrs. Jeepers walked in. The third-graders followed, staying as far from the giant as possible.

"Did you see that waffle face?" Eddie whispered when they were inside the entrance hall.

Howie nodded. "He has more scars than I have freckles."

"He's so tall," Melody whispered. "I've never seen anyone that big before."

The big man led them down a dark hall. Science exhibits filled the rooms on both sides. Tables covered with rocks lined the hall, and huge posters of labeled rocks covered the cracked walls.

"I could have stayed in my driveway and had more fun playing with the gravel," Eddie fussed.

"Quit complaining, Eddie," Melody snapped. "You know you'd rather be here than at school doing math."

"Math is starting to look better and better," Eddie whispered as they were led into a room full of mummies.

A small man in a white jacket greeted them. "That will be all, Frank. You have work to do elsewhere in the museum."

"Hrrmm." Frank glared down at the children once more before disappearing down a dark hallway.

The small man greeted the students, his eyes darting from face to face. "Welcome to the Shelley Museum. I am

the museum curator, Dr. Victor. And I see you've already met my assistant, Frank. I am looking forward to showing you the museum. I think you will be amazed."

"I think it's already amazing," Eddie whispered.

"What do you mean?" asked Howie.

"It's incredible that a weasel and a giant run a museum!"

"It's more incredible than you think," Liza muttered to her friends as the rest of the class followed Dr. Victor into the next room. "I have to tell you something."

"What's your problem?" Eddie asked.

"You have been acting strange," Melody said. "What's wrong?"

"You'll just laugh," Liza said.

"No, we won't." Melody gave Eddie a dirty look. "Will we, Eddie?"

Eddie rolled his eyes. "Nothing she says surprises me."

14

The three kids huddled around Liza. "My older brother had to read a book for an English report," Liza said softly. "He read it to me to scare me."

"Book reports scare me, too," Eddie snickered.

Liza shook her head. "I wasn't scared. At least not then, because it didn't seem real. But now it does."

"What was the book about?" Howie asked.

Liza took a shaky breath and began. "Long ago, a young scientist started secret experiments. He sneaked into cemeteries late at night to steal what he needed. Then he worked hundreds of hours putting his creation together."

Liza paused. Outside, the wind hissed, and a tree limb scraped against a window. The kids jumped, and then looked back at Liza.

"What was the creation?" Howie whispered.

"It was a monster brought back from the dead."

"That's disgusting," Melody said.

Eddie slapped Liza on the back. "I think it's cool."

"But it wasn't," Liza told him. "The scientist was afraid of his own creation. He fled, and the monster was forced to fend for himself."

"A monster ought to be able to take care of himself," Eddie said. "I do it all the time."

Liza shook her head. "It's easy for you. You're only half as hideous as the monster."

"That's a matter of opinion," Melody joked.

"What happened to the monster?" Howie interrupted.

"For a while, he roamed through the woods. He loved nature, especially flowers. But when people saw him they were so frightened, they tried to kill

16

him. He was deathly afraid of fire, and people chased him with torches. The monster had no choice. He had to kill — or be killed."

"That's terrible," Melody said.

"What's the name of that story, anyway?" Howie asked.

Liza looked at her friends before answering. *"Frankenstein."*

"I saw that movie on the late show," Eddie said. "What does that have to do with this old museum?"

Liza spoke softly. "This museum looks just like a picture in the book."

"Then where's the monster?" Howie asked as thunder rumbled overhead.

Liza's face grew pale. "We just saw the monster. And his name is Frank."

4
Bubbles

"Your brain has more bubbles than this room," Eddie told Liza when they caught up with the rest of the class. The third-graders were at the Science Fun exhibit, making bubbles. Bubbles of all sizes filled the air.

"Liza, you're jumping to conclusions," Howie said. "This place is neat." He grabbed a wand and made a

bubble the size of a basketball.

"There aren't any monsters here." Melody giggled as she picked up a wand. "Look at my square bubble!"

"Check out the Bubble Head," Eddie said as he covered Liza with a huge bubble. Liza popped it and gave Eddie a shove. He landed with his hands in a big tub of soapy water.

Melody jumped out of Eddie's way. "All this water reminds me that I have to find a bathroom. Come with me, Liza."

Liza looked down the dark hall. "I don't want to go. Besides, I'm making a star bubble."

"If you don't come right now, you'll be seeing stars," Melody insisted.

Thunder boomed as the girls headed down a dark hall. They peeked into several rooms full of display cases. Finally, Melody found a bathroom.

"Now, can we go back?" Liza asked.

Melody nodded. "I think it's this way."

"I thought it was that way!" Liza said, pointing the other way.

"No, we go *this* way," Melody said, "I'm sure."

"You're all mixed up," Liza said. "I

could swear the bubble room is back there."

Just then a crash came from where Liza was pointing.

"You're right," said Melody. "That must be Eddie."

The two girls made their way down the hall and pushed open a heavy door. What they saw made them gulp.

5
Planting Petunias

Spotlights lit up a small greenhouse connected to the museum. Red and purple petunias filled the greenhouse. Sweet-smelling roses and huge purple orchids were mixed in with the petunias making a sea of brilliant blossoms.

Frank towered over the colorful plants. Very gently, he pushed the lush green leaves aside to spray the soil with water from a water gun.

"There's Howie's gun." Melody giggled. "Frank must really like flowers."

"Frankenstein's monster loved flowers, too," Liza whispered.

"Shhh," Melody warned. "He heard you!"

"Hrrmm," Frank growled and faced

the girls. Then he lunged at them with the gun still in his hand.

"Let's get out of here before he catches us!" Liza squealed and fled down the hall.

"Hrrmm," Frank grunted and came after them. The floor shook with each step he took.

"We're going to die just because *you* had to go to the bathroom," Liza said as they raced away.

"Shut up and run faster," Melody yelled as they rounded a corner.

Plop! They ran smack into Howie and Eddie. "Aren't you girls a little late for the Indianapolis 500?" Eddie asked.

"Where have you been?" Howie asked.

"Never mind that," Melody shrieked. "Frank's after us. Run for your lives!"

"Here he comes!" Liza yelled.

"Hrrmm. *Hrrmm!*" The four kids

raced away from the giant until they came to a dead-end hall.

"Now what do we do?" Liza cried.

"We play pick a door." Eddie pointed to the three closed doors in the hallway. "Do you choose door number one, number two, or number three?"

"Door number three," Melody said, and the four scooted into the room just as they heard Frank coming down the hall. Liza bit her lip, and Melody crossed her fingers. Nobody breathed until Frank's groans faded away.

"Whew. That was too close." Liza sighed.

"Why was old hot dog breath chasing you, anyway?" Eddie asked.

"I don't know," Liza admitted. "But did you happen to notice where we are?"

The four kids stared at the brightly lit room. It was dark outside the window, but inside the room sparkled. Bright white cabinets brimming with crystal-clean glass beakers lined the walls. Strange equipment sat on the counters, and a long table was near a window. A funny odor filled the room.

"It looks like my dad's laboratory," Howie told them.

"I have a weird feeling about this," Liza whispered as lightning streaked across the sky.

6
Eyeball Stew

"You'd have a weird feeling about Beenie Weenies." Eddie laughed.

Howie picked up a beaker full of foaming ooze. "Liza may have a point. Look at this."

Eddie reached for the beaker. "Great. I was a little thirsty."

"Don't drink that," Liza squealed.

"I was just joking," Eddie snapped.

"Quit kidding around and come over here," Melody interrupted. She pointed to an enormous silver door.

Eddie shrugged. "Big deal. It's just a walk-in refrigerator. They have those at the Burger Doodle restaurant."

"Why would anyone need such a big

refrigerator in a laboratory?" Howie wondered out loud.

"Why would Dr. Victor need a laboratory in the first place? After all, this is a museum," Melody said. "And why would he keep his refrigerator locked?"

"Maybe he's working on creating another Frankenstein monster," Liza murmured as lightning flashed outside.

"Liza, if you had a brain you'd be dangerous." Eddie slapped the large silver refrigerator door.

"Maybe that's what's in this refrigerator," Melody told them.

"What?" Howie asked.

"Brains. And other body parts," Melody said.

"I've heard of brain sandwiches before, but that's disgusting," Howie said.

"How about finger sandwiches and eyeball stew," Eddie giggled.

"I bet you're right," Liza nodded.

Eddie pretended to throw up. "You

think Dr. Victor eats eyeball stew?"

"No, spaghetti brains," Liza snapped. "I think Dr. Victor is really Dr. Victor Frankenstein and he uses body parts to make monsters."

Eddie laughed. "I wish you'd get this Frankenstein business out of *your* brain."

No one noticed that the laboratory door had slowly opened behind them as Eddie laughed. Thunder shook the old museum, and then the lights went dead.

7
Hobby

"Aahhh!" Liza screamed and grabbed Eddie's arm. "What happened?"

Eddie knocked Liza's arm away. "The storm caused the lights to go out. There's no reason to squeeze the life out of me."

"We'll never find our way back in the dark," Melody gulped.

The laboratory was so dark, the four kids couldn't see their hands in front of them.

"Did you hear that?" Liza squealed. "It sounded like knuckles cracking!"

"Maybe it was some leftover fingers in the refrigerator getting some exercise." Eddie laughed.

"There's nothing funny about monsters living near Bailey City." Liza would've kicked Eddie's leg, but she couldn't find one in the dark.

"Speaking of monsters," a voice behind them said, "what are you third-grade monsters doing in my lab?"

"It's Dr. Victor," Melody gulped again.

Dr. Victor switched on a flashlight. The weak beam of light glowed on his face, making his eyes look like dark holes.

"Don't they teach you to read at Bailey Elementary?" Dr. Victor shined the flashlight on the open laboratory door. Big red letters spelled PRIVATE — DO NOT ENTER.

"We didn't see the sign," Melody apologized.

"We're s-s-sorry," Howie stammered. "We g-g-got lost."

Dr. Victor cracked his knuckles. "It is safest to stay with your teacher."

"Why?" Eddie blurted.

Dr. Victor smiled. His teeth were bright in the flashlight beam. "These halls are confusing. You might easily be lost in the museum for hours. It could be most unfortunate."

"Especially with a monster lurking in the shadows," Liza mumbled.

Dr. Victor glared at her before continuing. "Mrs. Jeepers has been very worried. If you will follow me I will take you to her and we will end this unfortunate incident."

"We would appreciate that," Howie said.

"And I would appreciate it if you would put this laboratory out of your mind," Dr. Victor said as he led them down the hall. "It has long been a hobby of mine to tinker in a lab, and I would like to keep it private."

"We understand," Melody told him. "Everybody has hobbies. I like to collect stamps."

"But very few people collect monsters," Liza muttered to herself as she followed Dr. Victor down the long dark hallway.

8
Big Bones

"I am disappointed in your behavior," Mrs. Jeepers told the four kids. Dr. Victor had taken them to the dinosaur exhibit. The rest of the class was sitting on benches beside huge replicas of a tyrannosaurus rex and an apatosaurus. Mrs. Jeepers and some of the kids were holding flashlights.

"I'm sorry," Melody explained. "I had to go to the bathroom."

"And then we got lost," Liza added.

Mrs. Jeepers rubbed her brooch and flashed her green eyes. "Do not let it happen again. As for our field trip, we may have to postpone the rest of the museum until the lights come back on."

"No need for that," Dr. Victor said.

"One charming thing about old buildings is that there are always plenty of candles." He held up a huge flaming candelabra. The light from the candelabra cast eerie shadows behind the life-sized dinosaur statues.

"Please explore to your heart's desire." Dr. Victor smiled.

"All right!" Eddie cheered and grabbed a plastic dinosaur bone the size of a broom. "If I had bones this size, nobody would mess with me."

"That is very true," Dr. Victor told him. "I have always thought that a larger species of humans would make the world a better place." He placed one candelabra next to the bone table. "Now, I must light more candles." Dr. Victor disappeared behind a group of third-graders.

"Did you hear that?" Liza squealed. "He wants all human beings to be bigger . . . just like Frank."

"Maybe he's trying to make an improved race of large people," Howie said.

Eddie laughed. "Frank is no monster. He's a great big museum assistant. Just because he's tall doesn't mean he's Dr. Victor's chemical creation brought back from the dead. If that were true, basketball players would be monsters, too."

"It's not that he's tall," Liza told them. "Haven't you noticed his scars?"

Melody nodded. "And Frank likes flowers. Just like Frankenstein's monster."

"You guys have flipped." Eddie laughed. "I saw the movie, and I'm sure of one thing. Frankenstein doesn't plant petunias." Eddie rolled his eyes. "Frank isn't Frankenstein's monster any more than I am."

"Mrs. DeeDee might not agree with you," Melody giggled. Mrs. DeeDee was a teacher who had quit just three weeks after teaching Eddie.

"Very funny," Eddie smirked. "I know Frank isn't the monster and I can prove it."

"How?" Liza asked.

But Eddie didn't get a chance to answer.

9

I Am Not a Man

"*Hrrmm!*" Frank stood near the door of the dinosaur room, staring at the candelabra. "HRRMM!" he bellowed again and backed up against the skeleton of a stegosaurus. The skeleton clattered to the floor as Frank ran from the room.

"It's the candelabra," Melody whispered. "He's afraid of fire."

Liza nodded. "Just like Frankenstein's monster."

Dr. Victor rushed into the room and set two more candelabras on the table. Then he kicked the stegosaurus bones into a heap. "Please excuse my assistant's behavior. He has not been well."

Mrs. Jeepers smiled her odd little half smile. "That is quite all right."

"Please, continue enjoying the dinosaur exhibit," Dr. Victor said. "I will see about finding more lights."

"It's just like a monster to destroy an entire skeleton," Liza whispered to her friends as Dr. Victor left the room.

"I told you," Eddie snapped. "Frank isn't a monster."

"How can you prove it?" Liza asked Eddie.

"There's got to be a way," Eddie shrugged. "I could ask him. 'Oh, by the way, Frank. Are you a Frankenstein monster?'"

"Right. One grunt would mean yes, and two grunts would mean no." Melody giggled.

"Shhh," Howie hissed. "Did you hear that?"

The four kids listened. Outside the museum, rain continued to pound the windows, and the wind howled around the old building.

"All I hear is the storm," Melody said.

"It's a doozy of a storm," Eddie agreed.

Liza shuddered. "I hope the bus can make it back to pick us up. I'd hate to be stuck here."

Crash!

"Now did you hear it?" Howie asked.

The third-graders stopped their exploring to listen. CRASH! CRASH! CRASH!

"It sounds like the building is falling apart," Howie said.

Liza gulped. "Maybe Frank is going

crazy and destroying the whole museum. Just like this poor skeleton."

"Where is Dr. Victor, anyway?" Melody wondered. "After all. This is *his* museum."

Mrs. Jeepers spoke calmly to the class and pointed down the hall. "The sound is coming from there. Stay here. I will check on the problem."

Mrs. Jeepers slowly walked down the dark hall toward the horrible sounds. Her small flashlight wavered in the shadows.

"We can't let her go alone," Melody told them.

"Why not?" Eddie asked. "If she is a vampire, nothing can hurt her. We, on the other hand, could be killed very easily."

"Eddie, for once in your life, be a man and help." Melody grabbed a candelabra from the table.

"In case you haven't noticed, I'm only

43

four foot three inches tall and in the third grade. I am not a man."

"I thought you wanted to prove Frank wasn't a monster," Melody said.

"I do," Eddie snapped as more crashes came from down the hall. "But Mrs. Jeepers told us to stay here."

"Since when do you do what Mrs. Jeepers wants?" Melody asked.

Howie threw back his shoulders and said bravely, "I'll go with you."

"Me, too," Liza squeaked a little less bravely.

Eddie snatched a flashlight from one of the other third-graders. "All right, I'll go. But I think you guys need to learn more about self-survival." Eddie led the way down the dark hall. Liza walked behind Melody, holding tightly to her arm.

CRASH! "It's coming from behind that door," Melody said.

"Well, open it," Eddie said.

"All right, scaredy-cat, I will." Melody slowly reached out her hand to turn the doorknob.

CRASH! The four kids jumped away from the door. "Maybe we better let Mrs. Jeepers handle this. After all, she is the teacher," Liza squeaked.

"Don't chicken out now," Melody said. She took a deep breath and quickly opened the door.

"Oh, my gosh," Liza screamed. "It's the end of the world!"

10
Greenhouse

"Get a grip on yourself," Eddie hollered. "It's just a storm." Wind whipped past the four kids as they stared into the greenhouse. One entire section of the wall had been ripped away, and rain was pouring onto the tiled floor. Large plants were scattered all over.

Liza screamed and pointed to the far corner where Mrs. Jeepers lay in a heap. "She's hurt." Before her friends could stop her, Liza rushed into the ruined greenhouse. Hail the size of lemons pelted the glass walls and roof of the room. Liza knelt beside Mrs. Jeepers and gently patted her hand. "Wake up, Mrs. Jeepers," she said.

"We better help before she's pulverized by hail," Melody said.

"I think someone else is going to pulverize both of them." Eddie gulped.

Frank appeared through the back door of the greenhouse. He towered over Liza and Mrs. Jeepers. Then he looked around and groaned. "Hrrmm. Hrrmm."

"He's going to kill Liza and Mrs. Jeepers," Howie screamed above the roar of the rain. "They're trapped like flies in a fly trap!"

"*Hrrmm!*" Frank growled at the kids. He took one step toward them, but a huge gust of wind tore the door off its hinges, taking part of the greenhouse wall with it. Frank cried and covered his face as pots of petunias flew past him.

"*Hrrmm!*" He dropped to the ground and crawled after his plants. Rain tore at his white shirt as the wind ripped a plant from his grasp. He struggled to grab more petunias as they blew past him.

"He's trying to save his plants," Melody said.

"Poor Frank," Liza cried. "He's losing his beautiful flowers."

"Poor Frank, nothing," Eddie said.

Suddenly part of the greenhouse roof started to squeak and crack. Frank looked up as it began to fall on Liza and Mrs. Jeepers.

"It's going to kill them!" Howie screamed.

But before the roof smashed to the floor, Frank lunged.

11
Ruined

Frank threw himself over Liza and Mrs. Jeepers, and they all disappeared under a pile of wooden beams.

"I don't believe it!" Eddie yelled. "Frank tried to save their lives."

"Are they alive?" Melody whispered as they made their way over the shattered roof and crushed plants.

When they found Liza and Mrs. Jeepers, Frank was leaning against the wall.

Liza smiled at the giant as she helped Mrs. Jeepers sit up. "Thank you for saving us. Now we'll help you save your petunias."

Before her friends could stop her, Liza chased a purple petunia.

The rain slowed to a steady drizzle as Liza and her friends helped collect the scattered plants. They had just filled a potting table with large red petunias when Dr. Victor rushed into the green-house.

"What have you little monsters done now?" he screamed.

Mrs. Jeepers calmly touched her brooch. "The children are helping Frank clean up the damage from the storm. Third-graders from Bailey Elementary are *not* monsters."

"Pardon me," Dr. Victor apologized and cracked his knuckles. "It is kind of you to help. Frank loves his flowers so."

Dr. Victor picked up a flowerpot and examined the large blossom. As he looked around the greenhouse, the petunia slipped through his fingers and smashed to the floor. Dr. Victor kicked several other plants out of the way as he ran to the destroyed side of the greenhouse. "No, Frank," Dr. Victor cried. "Please tell me you didn't."

He picked up a broken bottle with a large red label. The label read FORMULA BIG. He held the bottle upside down. One green liquid drop oozed out.

"Frank, why did you bring my formula in here?" Dr. Victor's voice was shaky. "Fourteen years of work, ruined. Ruined!" He put his face in his hands and slipped to the floor, sobbing.

Mrs. Jeepers quietly ushered the third-graders out of the greenhouse. "I think Dr. Victor needs some privacy," she said softly.

Liza took one last look at the greenhouse as she went into the museum. Broken pots, glass, and stray flowers

still covered the floor. As the last drops of rain fell, sunlight shone on Frank cradling Dr. Victor in his arms. Frank groaned as Dr. Victor sobbed. "Ruined, Frank. My hopes for you ruined."

12
Good-bye — For Now!

Mrs. Jeepers and the kids walked down the wet museum steps toward the school bus. The sun peeked through clouds as Frank appeared in the open museum door, his arms full of huge red petunias. He clomped down the steps toward the kids. "Hrrmm."

"I think he wants us to have the plants," Liza said as she took a pot from Frank. Each of her friends took one, too.

"These flowers are beautiful," Melody said.

"They're the prettiest ones I've ever seen," Howie agreed. "And the largest."

"That formula must really work," Eddie mumbled.

"Thank you, Frank," Liza said softly. "For the flowers — and for saving my life."

Frank blushed and looked down at the ground as the kids climbed onto the bus.

"You never did prove Frank wasn't a monster," Liza told Eddie as they drove away.

"Frank can't be a monster," Melody said.

"Why not?" Howie asked.

"Because Bailey City already has a monster." Melody giggled.

"It does?" Eddie asked.

"Yeah," Melody told her friends. "And his name is Eddie!"

Aliens
Don't Wear
Braces

1

Power Surge

Howie hung his purple bookbag in his third-grade classroom at Bailey Elementary School. "Did you study for the science test?" he asked his friend Eddie.

Eddie scratched his curly red hair and dropped his bookbag on the floor. "Naw. Who needs science, anyway?"

"I like science," Howie told him. "Especially when it's about outer space."

"You would. You have plenty of empty space between your ears." Eddie laughed and headed for his seat.

The other kids in the class were busy copying math problems from the board. School had not even started and Mrs. Jeepers, their teacher, already had everyone working!

There was something strange about

their third-grade teacher. Mrs. Jeepers was from the Transylvanian Alps and some kids thought she was a vampire. Her long hair was the color of a jack-o'-lantern, and a bat bracelet hung from her wrist. She always wore a huge green brooch and when she got mad, it glowed. Mrs. Jeepers had a way of flashing her green eyes that made kids think twice about causing trouble.

Eddie slid into his seat and tore a piece of paper from his notebook. He was only halfway finished copying the math problems when Mrs. Jeepers spoke in her Transylvanian accent. "It is time to take the science test. Please clear off your desks."

Melody's seat was beside Eddie. She twirled one of her black pigtails. "I hope I get a good grade. Don't you?"

Carey was behind Melody. "I studied all weekend. I'm sure I'll get the highest grade."

Eddie shrugged. "Who cares?"

Liza, a girl in front of Eddie, turned to look at him. "You did study, didn't you? After all, this is a big test. I just hope my nose doesn't start bleeding." When Liza was really upset, her nose usually bled.

"I'll give you a bloody nose," Eddie kidded, holding up his fist.

Melody glared at Eddie and handed Liza a wad of tissues. "Leave Liza alone or I'll give you a bloody nose!"

Eddie didn't have time to answer because Mrs. Jeepers put a paper on his desk. "There will be no talking," she told the students. "You may begin."

Eddie looked at the first question. He swallowed hard and looked at the next question. He was searching the second page for something he could answer when he heard a noise.

It sounded like someone was playing a low note on a tuba. The hum grew louder

and louder until the windows rattled. Melody slapped her hands over her ears and Liza whimpered, "What is that?"

Suddenly, all the lights flickered and then went out.

2

Missing Teacher

Mrs. Jeepers' eyes flashed at the ceiling. Then she touched her brooch. The green pin glowed mysteriously. The lights flickered again, and then stayed on. "You may continue with your test," she said quietly, still looking at the ceiling.

Eddie turned around to talk to Howie. "What's going on?"

Howie held his finger to his lips. "Shhh."

But it was too late. Mrs Jeepers walked up to Eddie and scooped up his paper. "Talking during tests is not permitted," she said in her strange accent. "You must speak with Principal Davis."

Eddie's face turned bright red. "But I wasn't cheating."

Mrs. Jeepers touched her green brooch

again and her eyes flashed. Melody gasped and Liza closed her eyes. Would Mrs. Jeepers do something terrible to him? Eddie didn't wait to find out. He slid from his desk and stomped out of the room.

The principal's office was a wreck. The secretary was pushing buttons and yelling into the intercom system for the art teacher while a second-grade teacher was talking with Principal Davis. Twenty-eight second-graders wandered around the office, pulling stuff off the secretary's desk and playing tag with each other.

Eddie plopped into a chair to watch the excitement. A tall woman with long white hair sat next to him. She wore a white shirt with big silver buttons, black leggings, and black boots that came up above her knees. Her face was long and thin and whiter than chalk dust. She smiled at him, showing a mouth full of metal braces.

"You're too old to have braces," Eddie blurted.

The woman shrugged. "What makes you think I am old?"

"You have white hair," Eddie told her.

The tall woman smiled again. "My hair may not be the delightful color of Jupiter like yours, but where I come from some people think I look young. And people are never too old to wear braces." Then she looked at Principal Davis.

"Are you waiting to see the principal?" Eddie asked her. "Because if you are, it might be a while. This place is a zoo."

The tall woman frowned and looked around the room. "There are no animals here," she said.

"I don't mean a real zoo," Eddie started to explain.

"It does not matter," the strange woman interrupted and pulled some papers out of her briefcase. "I will not have to wait much longer."

The second-grade teacher was still talking to Principal Davis.

"But my students are supposed to have art now," she was saying. "Where could the art teacher be?"

Principal Davis shook his head. "Mr. Gibson's car is in the parking lot and I saw him earlier this morning. He must be somewhere. First there was that electrical power surge, and now the art teacher is missing. If only there was a substitute teacher who could teach the art classes!"

The lady winked at Eddie before she walked up to Principal Davis and handed him her papers. "Hello, my name is Mrs. Zork. I am looking for a teaching job."

Principal Davis' mouth dropped open as he looked at Mrs. Zork's papers. "Can you teach art?"

"Art is my specialty," she said. "As a matter of fact, where I come from, my pottery is displayed in the capital."

Principal Davis grinned and gestured to the kids running circles around his desk. "They're all yours, Mrs. Zork."

As soon as the tall woman left with the children, Principal Davis looked at his secretary. "That was lucky."

Eddie watched the tall woman walk down the hall and whispered, "I think it's creepy."

3

Mrs. Zork

When Eddie got back from the principal's office, his class was lining up for art.

"Did you get in trouble?" Howie asked softly.

"Naw. Principal Davis was too busy chasing second-graders," Eddie told him.

"Those flickering lights were weird," Howie whispered to Eddie. "Even Mrs. Jeepers thought so."

"Speaking of weird, you should see the new art teacher," Eddie said.

"New art teacher? What happened to Mr. Gibson?" Liza asked.

Eddie shrugged. "No one knows. Not even Principal Davis."

"You're lying," Melody said. "Teachers don't just disappear."

72

"They do at Bailey Elementary," Eddie snapped.

"What's strange about this new art teacher?" Howie interrupted.

"For one thing, she looks like she fell into a bag of flour," Eddie told them. "Her face is so white I bet her blood has been sucked dry by Count Dracula."

"Maybe Mrs. Jeepers got her," Melody giggled.

"I think Eddie's exaggerating," Liza told her.

"You'll find out when you see her," Eddie told his friends as they left their classroom.

"I beg your pardon," Mrs. Jeepers said when she opened the art room door. "I am looking for Mr. Gibson."

The tall woman smiled at the class. The kids stared at her white face and silver braces. "I am the substitute, Mrs. Zork."

Mrs. Jeepers flashed her eyes. "But

I am certain I saw Mr. Gibson this morning. He did not say anything about leaving."

"Maybe he's sick," Liza blurted.

Mrs. Zork spoke so softly they had to strain to hear. "Mr Gibson had to leave . . . unexpectedly."

Mrs. Jeepers nodded. "I am sure no one will give Mrs. Zork any trouble." She looked straight at Eddie before she left.

The kids sat down at the paint-stained tables. "I am pleased to visit your school," Mrs. Zork told them. "I look forward to learning much from you."

"Don't you mean that we're going to learn from you?" Carey asked.

"But, of course," Mrs. Zork said softly. "We shall begin by having a pottery lesson."

"But what about the totem poles we were making?" Liza asked.

"Totem poles?" Mrs. Zork asked. "I know nothing about totem poles. But I am quite the expert at throwing clay pots."

Eddie laughed. "I'm good at throwing stuff, too!"

Mrs. Zork flashed her braces at Eddie. "Then you may be the first to demonstrate!" Before Eddie could complain, Mrs. Zork grabbed his hand and plopped a big blob of clay in front of him.

The clay was on a small table. Mrs. Zork pushed a button with her foot and the table began to whirl. Mrs. Zork held Eddie's hands in the clay and together they began forming a pot.

"That's neat," Liza said. "May I try?"

"Certainly." Mrs. Zork let go of Eddie's hands. Eddie quickly slipped away from the table and Liza took his place.

Liza pressed hard on the clay blob as the table whirled around. "I can't get it right," she complained.

"Yours looks like a hamburger," Carey said.

"Looks more like a flying saucer to me," Howie giggled.

"Do you mean an interplanetary transportation system?" Mrs. Zork asked.

Howie nodded. "I know all about spaceships. My dad works at the Federal Aeronautics Technology Station and he has all kinds of books about space."

Mrs. Zork's braces seemed to glow when she smiled at Howie. "That is very interesting information."

"FATS is where all the space nerds work," Eddie muttered, flicking little blobs of clay across the room.

"This is messy," Liza interrupted. Her hands were covered with slimy gray clay.

Melody laughed. "That's because you're all thumbs!"

Mrs Zork's braces sparked as she grabbed Liza's hands. "This child is not all thumbs," she said softly. "Her hands are just as human hands should be."

All the kids laughed.

"Quit laughing at me," Liza stammered.

"Don't get upset," Melody told her friend. "Your nose will start bleeding." But it was too late. Liza pulled a tissue from her pocket to stop the bleeding.

"What happened?" Mrs. Zork asked. "What's that red stuff?"

"My nose is bleeding," Liza told her, and showed her the tissue.

Mrs. Zork jumped back and looked at the blood-splattered table. "Oh my goodness! We must get you to the nurse right away."

The kids watched Mrs. Zork take Liza from the room. "She acted like she'd never seen blood before," Howie whispered.

"At least not red blood," Melody said.

ZING. A gray blob flew past Howie's head and splatted against the concrete wall.

"What was that?" Howie yelped.

"I just made one of your famous flying saucers," Eddie laughed. Then he snatched another glob of clay. "I can make more, too!"

Howie grabbed the clay. "Give me that!"

"This is our chance to have some fun," Eddie said, taking a green paint can off the shelf. "Let's spray paint the windows while Mrs. Zork is gone." Eddie squirted a white blob of paint on the nearest window. "Hey! Somebody switched the labels. This is supposed to be green."

Howie grabbed the can from Eddie. "Quit that, you moron. This is our chance to find out what happened to Mr. Gibson."

"What do you think you'll find?" Eddie laughed. "A tied-up art teacher in the filing cabinet?"

"Of course not," Melody interrupted. "But we might find a clue." With that the three children started peeping in cupboards and boxes. The rest of the third-graders were busy making clay pots.

Melody pointed to Mrs. Zork's open briefcase. "Look at this!"

"It's just an old newspaper," Eddie said.

Melody nodded. "It's a ten-year-old article about an alien space craft."

"Maybe she collects old newspapers to line her bird cage with," Eddie said.

"Then how do you explain this?" Howie asked as he pulled another paper from the briefcase.

"Easy," Eddie said. "It's a map. You can line a bird cage with those, too."

"That's not any map," Melody said. "It's a star map."

Howie nodded. "And somebody's charted a course on it."

"Some kid was probably playing connect-the-dots with the stars," Eddie laughed.

"Maybe," Howie said. "Or maybe somebody was making travel plans."

"That's silly," Melody giggled. "Nobody travels in space."

"Nobody," Howie said slowly, "except aliens."

4

The Surprise of Their Lives

Right after art class, Mrs. Jeepers took the third-graders to recess.

"Phe-ew," Melody said when they walked out the door. "It smells like burnt rubber."

"If you'd take a bath once in a while, maybe it wouldn't stink so bad," Eddie laughed.

"It smells just like my dad's lab coat," Howie said.

"Then maybe he needs a bath, too," Eddie said as he ran to the huge oak tree in the playground. His friends followed him to their usual meeting place.

Eddie hung upside down from a branch and blew spit bubbles. "You're strange, Eddie," Melody told him.

"What's really strange is that art teacher," Howie said.

Eddie jumped down from the tree. "I could've sworn she had dull metal braces when I saw her in the office. But they looked really shiny in art class."

"Maybe she cleaned them," Melody said.

Howie shook his head. "But don't you think it's odd the way she came out of nowhere? And don't forget Mr. Gibson's disappearance!"

"She's just a crazy art teacher. Come on, I'll show you," Eddie bragged as he walked away.

"Where are we going?" Liza squeaked.

"We're going to spy on her. And if you don't come, that means you're a chicken!" Eddie told them.

The four kids sneaked around the building to the art room window. They had to stand on tiptoes to peek inside. Mrs. Zork stood in front of the classroom television.

She was watching Melody's favorite cartoon, *Puddle Blasters.*

"I love this part," Melody whispered. "This is where Puddle Man turns the desert into a huge flower garden."

"Look at all those pretty pink flowers," Liza sighed.

"Mrs. Zork likes them," Howie said as Mrs. Zork reached out and touched the flowers. When she did, her long white hair started to move.

"The static in the TV is making her hair stick straight up," Eddie laughed. "She looks like the Bride of Frankenstein."

"Something's wrong," Liza interrupted. "The flowers are fading." She was right. The bright cartoon petunias were soon black and white.

"The TV must be broken," Melody shrugged.

"I'm not so sure," Howie said slowly. But before they could say more, Mrs.

Zork turned in their direction. A pink streak of light flashed from her braces.

"Let's get out of here!" Howie yelled. The four kids raced around the building. They were panting when they reached the oak tree.

"Why did you run?" Eddie snapped.

Howie faced his friends. "Didn't you see how her braces turned pink?"

Eddie shrugged. "It was just the sun shining on them."

"Then explain why the pink flowers in the cartoon faded."

His three friends laughed at Howie. "Because it's an old TV," Melody told him.

Howie looked at his friends. Then he spoke very slowly. "That old newspaper article and star map reminded me of something I heard my dad talk about with the scientists from the Federal Aeronautics Technology Station."

Eddie laughed. "Those scientists at FATS spend all their time talking about aliens and flying saucers."

"Exactly," Howie whispered. "I think Mrs. Zork is an alien."

His three friends laughed.

"Aliens are little green men with antennas," Eddie snickered.

Melody nodded. "They don't just land their flying saucers on the playground and decide to be art teachers!"

"And they definitely don't wear braces," Liza giggled.

Howie pointed his finger at his friends. "Remember when the lights went on and off this morning?"

"What about it?" Eddie asked.

"That was probably when she landed. This awful smell is from the spaceship's fumes."

"Next you'll tell us Carey is the Star Fleet Commander." Melody giggled so hard she had to sit down on the ground.

"You can laugh if you want," Howie warned his friends. "But I think Bailey Elementary needs to watch out for Mrs. Zork."

5

UFO

Howie waved a newspaper at his three friends. "Look at these headlines. They're all about flying saucers here in Bailey City." It was the next morning, and the four kids were gathered at their usual meeting place. Bright yellow dandelions surrounded the big oak tree. Eddie kicked a yellow dandelion before grabbing the newspaper to glance at the headlines. "UFOs. Ugly Fat Omelets," he laughed. "There's no such thing as flying saucers."

"You may not believe in Unidentified Flying Objects," Howie said slowly, "but my dad has plenty of books that tell all about them."

"People write books about ghosts, too," Eddie said. "And there's no such thing."

"Well, a lot of people around here do

believe in UFOs," Howie pointed out. "As a matter of fact, there was a famous sighting right here in Bailey City, just ten years ago."

"Yeah, by some nearsighted granny who spotted Principal Davis' bald head shining in the sun," Eddie laughed.

"The article I saw in Mrs. Zork's briefcase was from ten years ago," Melody said slowly.

Howie nodded. "That's the case I'm talking about. The scientists at FATS documented the case."

"Did your dad tell you that?" Liza asked.

"I overheard my dad talking on the phone when I was visiting him last weekend," Howie told her. "When I asked him about it, he wouldn't say anything else. I think it might have something to do with Mrs. Zork. If you promise not to tell a soul, I'll tell you what I heard."

Liza and Melody nodded.

"What about you?" Howie asked Eddie. "Do you promise?"

Eddie shrugged. "Who would I tell?"

The four friends huddled under the oak tree. "Ten years ago," Howie began, "an alien spacecraft was sighted near Bailey City. During the following week, all the flowers faded and died."

"You're making this up," Eddie interrupted. "If that was true, Bailey City would be world famous for their museum of little green men."

Howie shook his head. "It's top secret. The government denies it ever happened because it would cause mass hysteria."

Eddie laughed. "Sounds hysterical to me."

Melody nodded. "Everyone knows the flowers died because the Red River dried up. Besides, if the aliens haven't come back for ten years, why would they come now?" she asked.

"That's what my dad was talking about

on the phone. It has something to do with the alignment of the planets," Howie said. "It's exactly the same as ten years ago. I think the aliens have returned to Bailey City, and Mrs. Zork is one of them."

"I think you have wet noodles for brains," Eddie laughed. With that, he ran into school. The other three kids shrugged as they followed him into the building. But they all froze when they saw Mrs. Zork and Mrs. Jeepers talking in the hall.

Mrs. Zork's hair looked more blonde than white, and her cheeks were pink. "What a lovely pin," she said as she touched the brooch Mrs. Jeepers always wore. "It is such a nice shade of green. I wish we had pins this color where I am from."

Mrs. Jeepers stepped away from the new art teacher. "Thank you very much," she said softly. "It is very special."

Mrs. Zork nodded. "It highlights your beautiful red hair."

Mrs. Jeepers glanced at Mrs. Zork, but her eyes didn't flash like they usually did.

The four kids followed Mrs. Jeepers into the classroom. "Did you see Mrs. Zork's hair?" Melody whispered. "It's a different color."

"She probably dyed it," Eddie snapped.

"Well, I think she looks better with makeup," Melody told her friends. "She looked dead yesterday."

Howie nodded. "Mrs. Jeepers sure could use some of that makeup. She looks exhausted."

It was true. Mrs. Jeepers was pale and even her green eyes seemed dull. Her red hair lacked its usual shine and her brooch looked cloudy.

"Maybe she's sick," Eddie whispered. "I bet we can get away with stirring up some trouble."

Then Eddie went into action. While Carey sharpened her pencil, he drew a big red "F" on her homework paper. When Carey saw it she squealed, "Mrs. Jeepers! Eddie drew all over my homework! It's ruined."

The class held their breath as Mrs. Jeepers stood up from her desk. She glared at Eddie and then slowly rubbed her brooch.

Eddie waited for a split second and then grinned. "It's party time," he whispered under his breath. Then he hopped on his seat and did a little jig.

"Are you crazy?" Howie hissed as he pulled Eddie down. "She'll turn you into bat bait!"

Eddie shook his head. "She's lost it. She's lost her power. Just look at her."

All the kids stared at Mrs. Jeepers. They held their breath as she pulled the brooch off her starched white blouse.

When she saw the faded stone, she gasped. Without another word, Mrs. Jeepers rushed from the room.

6

Makeup Crazy

Eddie didn't waste a second. As soon as Mrs. Jeepers left he ransacked her desk for tomorrow's homework answers. He ducked under the desk when Principal Davis popped his bald head in the door. "Students," he announced, "Mrs. Jeepers has taken ill. Line up at the door and I will take you to art."

As the kids followed Principal Davis out the door, Eddie sneaked to the end of the line. "I hope Mrs. Jeepers is going to be okay," Liza whispered to him.

"Mrs. Jeepers has never been okay," Eddie sneered. "I don't know why she would start now."

"I've never seen her act like that," Melody pointed out. "Something was terribly wrong with her brooch."

"It was fading," Howie murmured. The four kids were quiet as Principal Davis looked back at him. As he walked in silence, Howie noticed the artwork in the hall. Brightly colored clown pictures were stapled on a cork strip lining the hallway. Howie looked at each picture. The closer he got to the art room, the more faded the clowns looked.

"Weren't these pictures brighter yesterday?" Howie wondered out loud.

"Shhh." Principal Davis gave him a stern look.

Howie bit his lip and walked quietly into the art room with his friends. When Mrs. Zork smiled at them, her braces glowed pink. Her lips were bright pink and it looked as if she had used a bottle of pink paint on her cheeks. Even her hair had an extra glow to it.

"Mrs. Zork must have started beauty school," Melody giggled under her breath.

"It looks like she drained the color from this room," Howie whispered. Melody, Liza, and Eddie looked around. The blackboard was gray, the construction paper was pale, and even the bottles of paint looked drab.

"It looks like Eddie poured brown paint over everything," Melody whispered.

"Don't look at me," Eddie muttered.

"You're right," Mrs. Zork interrupted. "Right now, you need to look at me. It is time for another pottery lesson. Do we have a volunteer?"

Everyone but Eddie, Melody, Howie, and Liza raised their hands. Mrs. Zork called on Carey. "I just love your bright pink sweatshirt. I wish I had something that color," she said as Carey grabbed a blob of clay. Howie's eyes grew wide as Mrs. Zork lightly touched the arm of Carey's shirt.

"What's the matter?" Eddie asked him.

"Tell you later," Howie said and moved

as far away from Mrs. Zork as he could.

Art class seemed to last forever. Howie had never been so glad to see Principal Davis' shiny head in all his life. "I'm taking you out for an early recess," Principal Davis told the class. He pretended not to notice the scramble behind him as everyone tried to be first in line. Everyone but Howie, that is.

"What's wrong with you?" Melody asked as they gathered under the oak tree. "You look like Superman just spit in your face."

"Didn't you notice anything on the way to the art room?" Howie asked.

"Yeah, I noticed Principal Davis' underwear was sticking out of his pants," Melody said rolling her eyes.

Howie shook his head. "I'm talking about all the pictures. They were faded."

"That's just the sun," Liza piped up. "It

always fades stuff that's hanging."

"Didn't the art room look different to you?" Howie asked.

"It's the same stupid art room," Eddie shrugged. "Only now it's got a makeup-crazy substitute in it."

"I don't think she's makeup crazy," Howie said. "I think she's color crazy."

"Huh?" Melody, Liza, and Eddie said together.

"Don't you remember Mrs. Zork touching Mrs. Jeepers' brooch this morning?" Howie said.

"So? Maybe she likes old jewelry," Melody said.

"Right after that, Mrs. Jeepers starting acting funny and her brooch looked different," Howie reminded them.

"Almost like it was losing its color!" Liza chimed in.

"And look at Carey's shirt." Howie pointed to the swings where Carey played. Her shirt was no longer as pink as bubble gum. Now it was a mucky brown.

"She must've splattered it with that yucky clay," Melody said.

"I don't think so," Howie said slowly. "It's fading just like the flowers faded ten years ago."

"What in the world are you talking about?" Eddie snapped.

"I'm talking about an alien stealing our colors," Howie whispered.

7
Green Cheese and Laser Guns

"Mrs. Zork is no alien and I can prove it," Eddie bragged.

"How?" Melody asked.

"Simple," Eddie told them. "I'll follow her home."

"What will that prove?" Liza asked.

Eddie kicked at a rock lying on the ground. "Any self-respecting alien is bound to have green cheese or laser guns lying around. I'll peek in her window and see that she's just an ordinary teacher."

"Isn't peeking into somebody's house against the law?" Liza asked.

Eddie shrugged. "I've peeked in plenty of windows before."

"I guess it is the only way to find out about Mrs. Zork," Melody agreed.

"We'll wait until she leaves," Eddie

told them. "Then we'll follow her home."

"I just hope she doesn't leave in a spaceship," Howie muttered.

After school the four kids hid behind the Dumpster. Soon Mrs. Zork rushed out of the school. Her braces sparkled bright pink when she glanced up at the sky.

"I bet she's looking for her spaceship," Howie whispered.

"Did you see her braces?" Liza squealed. "They changed colors again. Maybe she is an alien."

"Her braces probably measure all the color she's stolen," Howie told them.

"Naw. She's just a bad aim with her lipstick," Eddie said.

"Shhh," Melody warned. The four kids waited for Mrs. Zork to walk half a block before they followed cautiously. Mrs. Zork lived on Zender Street in a small white house with black shutters. Behind the tiny house was a gravel driveway

leading to an old rundown garage.

"She isn't an alien any more than you are," Eddie said when he saw Mrs. Zork's house.

"Don't be so sure," Howie told him. "Let's look around back." The four friends sneaked around the side of the house. A huge black satellite dish took up nearly half the backyard.

"There's proof," Howie hissed. "She's probably receiving secret messages from her mother ship in outer space."

Eddie rolled his eyes. "A lot of people have satellite dishes," he snapped. "Maybe Mrs. Zork likes to watch foreign films."

Howie glared at Eddie and then crept up to the garage windows with his three friends close behind. Without a word, they peered inside. What they saw took their breath away.

8

Great Martians Alive

Inside the dingy garage was a white dome that looked like a huge turtle shell. Pale pink and green lights blinked all around its base.

"Gosh!" Liza whispered.

"It can't be real," Melody insisted.

"There's only one way to find out," Eddie said. "I'm going in."

"You can't just walk into an alien's garage," Liza whispered. "You could get arrested for trespassing."

"Who'd arrest me?" Eddie snapped. "The space cadets?" He slowly turned the rusty doorknob. The door creaked open and Eddie slipped inside.

"I'm not going in there," Liza whimpered.

"We can't let him go alone," Howie

told her. He took a deep breath and followed his friend.

Melody started to go, but Liza grabbed her. "Don't leave me by myself!"

Melody pulled her arm away. "I'm not about to stay out here where Mrs. Zork can see us. It's safer inside. Now, come on!"

Eddie and Howie were already checking out the odd dome. A strange humming sound came from inside.

"That's the humming sound we heard at school," Liza gulped. "Just before the electricity went dead."

"It's got to be a spaceship," Howie whispered.

"I'll believe that when I see it zoom through the sky," Eddie told them.

"Maybe you'll believe this." Melody pointed to a color chart hanging on the wall next to a large panel of buttons. The word SPECIMENS was stamped on the top of the chart. The kids stared at the names listed down the side. Mrs. Jeepers' name was written in green, Carey's name in pink, and Eddie's name in red.

"Pink and green," Melody whispered. "Just like the blinking lights on this ship!"

"Why does she have my name in her garage?" Eddie asked.

Melody shrugged. "Maybe she's taking human souvenirs back to colonize new planets."

"But why are the names written in different colors?" Liza asked.

"I know!" Howie swallowed hard. "Every person listed on that chart has a color Mrs. Zork wants. She got the green from Mrs. Jeepers' brooch, and the pink from Carey's sweater! It's obvious she's stealing all our colors."

"Who cares about missing colors?" Eddie asked.

Howie pointed to the chart. "You should. Because I think your red hair is next!"

9

Alien Invasion

"Did you tell your dad?" Melody asked Howie the next morning. "Is he going to help us?"

"My father wouldn't believe me," Howie told his friends. They were standing under the oak tree on the playground. A cold breeze made the white dandelions shiver. "He thinks I'm crazy. He said I may need therapy."

Eddie punched Howie on the arm. "I always knew you needed a shrink."

"This is no laughing matter," Melody interrupted. "Bailey City is being invaded by aliens."

"One goofy art teacher does not make an invasion," Eddie said.

"Then explain these white dandelions,"

Howie said. "And the spaceship in her garage."

"Spaceship?" a soft voice came from behind.

"MRS. ZORK!" Liza squealed. "We didn't see you!"

The four friends faced the new art teacher. She was wearing a bright green jumpsuit with a pink scarf around her waist. A white dandelion was in her yellow hair.

Melody put her hands on her hips. "But we did see a spaceship in your garage."

Mrs. Zork frowned at the four children. Her braces sparked hot pink when she smiled. "You must mean my kiln. I use it for firing pottery."

"If that's a kiln, then I'm a monkey's uncle," Eddie told her.

Mrs. Zork slowly patted Eddie on his head. "Do not be silly. You look nothing like a monkey. Now you children must go to class."

The four kids followed Mrs. Zork into the building. "I told you it wasn't a space-ship," Eddie laughed. "It's just an oven for baking clay!"

"Maybe you're right," Liza said softly.

"Then what's happening to Eddie's hair?" Melody asked.

10

Drained

Eddie rushed to the bathroom to check his hair. "What are you talking about? I've still got my hair," Eddie snapped when he came out. "It's probably bleached from playing in the sun yesterday."

"She did it to you!" Melody said. "She stole your red hair."

"You can think what you want," Howie told Eddie. "But I know Mrs. Zork is stealing all our colors. And if we don't do something about it, we're doomed to live in a gray-and-white world."

Eddie laughed. "Who cares?"

Liza pointed inside their classroom. "You will care if we end up with Principal Davis as our substitute for the rest of the year."

Eddie groaned. Everybody knew that Principal Davis was the toughest teacher to ever hit an elementary school. His idea of fun was copying hundreds of math problems from the board. He was already busy filling up the board with double-digit multiplication problems.

"We haven't even learned that yet," Liza whimpered as they went into their room.

Principal Davis smiled from behind his glasses. "Then it's about time you did. I'm looking forward to teaching it to you today."

"Where's Mrs. Jeepers?" Melody asked. "Is she still sick?"

Principal Davis nodded. "She's feeling a little drained. She won't be back until her color is normal. I couldn't get a substitute teacher. So you're stuck with me. Luckily, we have plenty to keep us busy."

The class had no time to groan before they started copying math problems.

After that they did ten pages from their English book, seven pages from their social studies book, read three chapters from a funny story, and did every magnet experiment from their science book. And that was all before lunch!

By the time they reached the cafeteria, the kids looked as if they had run the Boston Marathon.

"I'm too tired to eat," Melody complained when she sat down with a tray.

"We'd better eat," Liza told them. "We need all our strength for this afternoon!"

"Principal Davis is working our fingers off," Eddie griped as he bit into a hot dog. "There's no telling what he'll make us do after lunch."

"Or tomorrow," Howie added, waving a french fry. "And the day after, and for the rest of the year."

"What do you mean?" Melody asked.

"Mrs. Jeepers is never coming back,"

Howie said slowly. "Not until we get her color back."

Eddie shook his head. "Why should we help? I never liked her anyway."

"We have to help her," Howie said softly. "Unless you want to be stuck with Principal Davis for the rest of the year."

Eddie swallowed hard and nodded. His voice was hoarse when he said, "We'll meet under the oak tree when it gets dark."

11

"We Know Who You Are"

Howie stood under the oak tree and checked his neon-orange glow-in-the-dark watch. The night air sent chills up his back, and the crooked branches of the oak tree made an eerie pattern against the starry sky. Finally, Eddie came jogging up the street.

"Where have you been?" Howie shivered and pulled his jacket tight.

"I had to wait for Dad to fall asleep," he answered. "Where are Liza and Melody?"

"I guess they couldn't make it," Howie said. "C'mon. Let's head for Mrs. Zork's place."

The two boys headed down Zender Street, making sure to stay in the shadows. The street was still and quiet. Many of the houses were brightly lit. The blue glow of TVs came from many of them, but Mrs. Zork's house was totally dark.

"Maybe nobody's home," Eddie whispered. "Let's go check out the garage." The two boys shivered in the night wind as they crept around back.

A low humming sound came from the strange object, and the blinking lights made eerie shadows on the wall. Howie pointed to the new row of red lights.

"There's the red from your hair. We have to get the colors out."

The two boys searched for an entrance to the object. "There's no opening," Howie said.

Eddie pointed to the panel of buttons on the side. "Maybe one of these will get it open." Then he started punching the buttons.

"Don't push those," Howie squeaked. "You don't know what you're doing."

It was too late. The top of the dome lifted up. But before they had a chance to look inside, they heard a soft voice behind them.

"What are you boys doing in my garage?" said a voice so quiet that Eddie could barely make out the words.

"We've come to save our colors," Howie said bravely.

Mrs. Zork laughed and her braces sparked in the dim light of the dome.

"We know who you are," Howie said, "and why you're here. We won't let you get away with it."

Mrs. Zork put a long skinny hand on Howie's neon-orange glow-in-the-dark watch. "Eddie, help me," Howie squeaked.

Eddie put his hand on a large black switch. "Let go of him, or I'll send your spaceship back into orbit."

"What?" Mrs. Zork said, holding fast to Howie.

"Maybe this will get your attention!" Eddie hollered and flipped the switch. A loud *ping* rang throughout the garage and the lights flickered.

"Stop that at once," Mrs. Zork demanded.

Eddie placed a finger on the blinking red button. "Not until you let Howie go."

Mrs. Zork's hand slipped away and

Howie quickly moved beside Eddie. "Make her let the colors out, too," Howie told Eddie.

"You heard him," Eddie said to Mrs. Zork. "Let them go. You have until the count of five, then I'm going to push this button."

"Stay away. Its very hot!" Mrs. Zork's braces sparked more than usual in the dark garage.

"One, two, three, four. . . ." Eddie counted. "Only one more and then your precious spaceship is spare parts."

Mrs. Zork's braces were a bright glowing red when Eddie hollered, "FIVE!" He leaned with all his might on the red button.

Red coils lit up and steam came from the bottom of the dome. The entire garage started shaking and a high-pitched squealing filled the air.

"That thing's going to explode!" Eddie screeched.

Howie grabbed Eddie's arm. "Let's get out of here before this whole garage blows up."

At the end of Zender Street they stopped to catch their breath. Over Mrs. Zork's house, a fountain of sparks arched high in the air like a burning rainbow.

12

Flu Season?

Melody was under the big oak tree the next morning picking a bright yellow dandelion when Howie and Eddie got there. "What happened at Mrs. Zork's last night?" she asked.

Howie looked at Eddie. They hadn't figured out what to tell their friends. Luckily, Liza skipped up to the tree and changed the subject. "Did you guys see those strange streaks of light in the sky last night?" she asked.

"It was probably the auto dealer having a sale," Melody said. "They always shine these big spotlights up in the sky. Once I thought one was a UFO!"

"It looked more like fireworks to me," Liza said. Then she looked at Eddie. "Your hair's bright red again!"

Eddie shrugged. "It's the same hair. It must be the way the sun is shining on it. I'm surprised it's not gray from all the work Principal Davis made us do yesterday."

"There's no telling what he has in store for us today," Melody groaned. "I guess we better head inside and find out."

Howie and Eddie were quiet as they walked into the classroom. They didn't know what to do about Mrs. Zork, but they both forgot all about her when they saw Mrs. Jeepers was back.

"Good morning, students," she said in her strange accent. She was wearing a crisp white blouse, and at her throat sparkled the bright green brooch.

"Were you sick?" Carey asked.

Mrs. Jeepers' eyes flashed, but then she smiled. "I was a little peaked, but I feel much better now. Unfortunately, I have some bad news. There was an explosion in Mrs. Zork's garage last night. It seems that her kiln went up in smoke."

"It went up all right," Eddie mumbled.

"Did you say something, Eddie?" Mrs. Jeepers asked as she touched her brooch.

"Uh . . . I said . . . is Mrs. Zork all right?" Eddie stammered.

Mrs. Jeepers smiled. "Luckily, no one was injured. However, Principal Davis was notified that there was quite a bit of damage done to her home, so she must move."

"Do you mean Mrs. Zork won't be coming back to Bailey Elementary?" Liza asked.

"I am afraid not," Mrs. Jeepers said. "But the good news is that Mr. Gibson is back with us after his bout with the flu. He was so ill, he slept through most of this week."

As the kids walked to art, they noticed new colorful pictures hanging on the walls. Even the pictures by the art room were bright and cheerful.

"We helped after all," Howie whispered to Eddie. "You must have released the colors when you pushed the red button."

"This is one time I'm glad everything is back to normal," Eddie said.

"Me, too," Liza sighed.

Melody nodded. "But things never stay normal for long at Bailey Elementary!"

Genies Don't Ride Bicycles

To Robert Edwin Thornton and Voline "Bonnie" Gibson.
Thanks for the bike rides
and bringing magic into our lives.

1

The Bottle

"What is it?" Melody asked Eddie. "Let me see."

"Keep your pigtails glued on," Eddie told her. "It's stuck." Eddie, Melody, and their friends Howie and Liza were in their favorite meeting place under the big oak tree on the school playground. The sun shone bright in the blue December sky, but none of the kids paid any attention. It was the first time they had noticed a strange object sticking out from a crack between two branches of the tree. Eddie tugged as hard as he could, but it didn't move.

Liza flung her blonde hair over her shoulder. "Maybe it's buried treasure."

"In a tree?" Eddie laughed.

"Let me help," Howie offered. Together the two boys tugged. All at once the object broke free and they fell backwards onto the ground.

Eddie held the object in his hands. "It's just an old bottle," he sighed as he looked at the slick green bottle. It had strange words scribbled across the side and a big gold stopper.

"Why don't you open it?" Liza asked. "Maybe someone put a secret message inside and it's been hidden for hundreds of years."

"If it's been hidden there for hundreds of years then why haven't we seen it before?" Eddie asked.

Melody nodded. "We're here every day after school. There's no way we could have missed it."

"It was hidden in that crack. Last night's windstorm probably loosened the tree limb," Howie suggested.

"If you're not going to open it, then

give it to me." Melody reached for the bottle.

"I'll open it." Eddie pulled on the gold stopper. It didn't budge. He sat down on the ground and put the bottle between his legs. He pulled again with all his strength.

POP!

"Pew-whee! What's that smell?" Liza complained.

Eddie stood up and held the bottle toward his friends. "It's this old bottle.

There's nothing in it except a sewer smell." He threw the bottle and the stopper into the yard next to the school.

"You shouldn't litter," Liza told him.

Eddie shrugged. "There's nothing in that yard but junk. One more stinky bottle won't make a difference."

The four kids looked at the yard behind the oak tree. A broken wooden fence surrounded flat tires, broken bottles, and metal barrels.

"It sure is ugly." Liza shivered and pulled on her mittens. "Especially when the other houses have bright Christmas lights."

"I wish someone would clean up this place," Melody said.

"You might as well wish for a million dollars," Eddie told her. "No one's lived in that dump for years."

Melody sighed. "You're right. But it never hurts to wish."

2

Holiday Spirit

"I can't believe it!" Howie shouted. "It was a junkyard yesterday." He was the first one to reach the oak tree the next day before school.

Melody trotted up beside him and stared. "It's a miracle!"

"It's a miracle Mrs. Jeepers hasn't driven me crazy. I thought I'd never finish my science homework." Eddie shook his head as he and Liza walked up to the oak tree. Mrs. Jeepers was their strict third-grade teacher.

"Mrs. Jeepers is nothing compared to this." Melody pointed to the yard next to the school. Yesterday the yard had been filled with trash, but today not a speck of broken glass or old tires remained.

Even the green bottle was gone. Now the grass was neatly trimmed and the fence was straight and covered with Christmas lights. Bright strands of lights were strung on the railing of the back porch and were draped around every tree and bush in the yard.

Liza had a long woolen scarf wrapped around her neck so only her nose and eyes could be seen. "It looks great," she said.

"It's great for the electric company," Eddie laughed. "Whoever hung those lights is going to have a doozie of an electric bill."

"I guess Melody was right," Liza said. "It never hurts to make a wish."

Howie looked at his friends. "Don't you think it's odd that this junkyard was cleaned up overnight?"

"I think it's wonderful," Liza said through her scarf.

Just then a big man with a shiny bald

head rode a purple bicycle into the yard behind the house. Muscles bulged under his gold brocade vest and bright, flowing orange pants covered his legs. Gold necklaces hung around his neck and one ear had a gold earring dangling from it. He honked the bicycle's horn and waved at the four friends. "How do you do?" he sang out in a deep voice.

"J . . . just fine, thank you," Howie answered. "How are you?"

The big man laughed a deep friendly laugh. "Today, I am fine. As a matter of fact, today I am wonderful. It's been ages since I've gotten any exercise."

"I haven't seen you around before," Eddie said suspiciously.

The man smiled. "I breezed in yesterday."

Liza reached out her hand. "My name is Liza. It's very nice to meet you."

The man leaned his bike against the fence and reached to kiss Liza's hand.

"My name is Eugene and it is my pleasure to serve such a lovely fair-haired lady."

Liza giggled. "You sure made this yard sparkle."

When the stranger laughed his teeth shone next to his dark skin. "I've been cooped up for such a long time it felt good to work in the fresh air."

Liza nodded. "I bet the rest of the neighbors will be glad! Finally this house has some holiday spirit!"

"I wish we didn't have to go to school," Eddie muttered as the school bell rang. "Then I'd have some holiday spirit, too."

As they turned to leave, Liza waved at Eugene. "We'll see you later," she said.

Eugene bowed. "Your wish is my command." His deep laughter echoed across the playground and followed the kids into the school.

3

Blizzard

Mrs. Jeepers, their third-grade teacher, rubbed her green brooch as Eddie, Liza, Melody, and Howie rushed to their seats.

"We're sorry to be late," Melody said.

Howie nodded. "We were just admiring the new neighbor's holiday decorations."

Mrs. Jeepers' green eyes flashed in their direction. "We do not have time to waste on twinkling lights." Mrs. Jeepers had a strange accent and spoke very softly. She didn't need to shout because the kids in her class always paid attention. If they didn't, she rubbed her brooch and her green eyes flashed. Then strange things would happen. Some kids even believed she was a vampire.

By the time Mrs. Jeepers loaded them down with work, the kids had forgotten all about the new neighbor. They were busy with fifty math problems and two science experiments.

Halfway through the morning, Howie blew on his hands to warm them, and Liza's teeth started chattering. Mrs. Jeepers pulled on a sweater and checked the thermostat.

"It's too cold in here to work," Melody whispered.

Eddie shrugged. "It's not so bad. It never gets real cold in Bailey City." But Eddie was wrong. By the end of the day, thick gray clouds rolled over the city, and ice formed on the windows of the school.

"Maybe it'll snow," Melody whispered as they turned in their English assignments.

Howie shook his head. "Bailey City has not had a decent snow in years.

Besides, I heard the weather report on the radio this morning. It is going to be sunny and mild today."

"Maybe in Hawaii, but it definitely looks like snow for Bailey City!" Eddie pointed out the window. Huge soft snowflakes drifted down and stuck to the bare branches of the old oak tree.

By the end of the school day, a white rug of snow completely covered the ground, and the big oak tree's branches looked like sticks with white cotton candy.

Eugene honked his bicycle horn when the kids rushed out of the school door. "How do you like the snow?" he asked, parking his bike. He was still dressed in his vest and flowing pants.

"It's beautiful!" Melody laughed and stuck out her hand to catch a snowflake.

Liza put on her hat and wrapped a scarf around her face as the kids slid across the playground. "We'd better hurry

home. The streets are going to get slippery."

"Great." Eddie skated on the slick snow behind Eugene's house. "The roads will be bad, and school will be canceled!"

"You will be in the holiday spirit now," Eugene hollered to Eddie.

Howie froze right in the middle of a step. "Did you hear that?" he asked.

"All I hear is Liza's teeth chattering," Eddie told him.

"I meant what Eugene said," Howie hissed. "It's what Eddie wished for."

"What are you talking about?" Melody asked.

"Eddie wished for no school."

"So, why complain?" Eddie asked.

"I'll tell you why," Melody interrupted. "Harry Headbanger and his band are supposed to play for us tomorrow. We'll miss it if the snow doesn't melt."

"That's just great," Eddie grumbled. "One good thing happens all year and we'll miss it because of this stupid snow."

Eugene kicked through the snow with his funny green boots and leaned on the fence. "Why so glum, my young friends? You said you did not want to go to school and it looks like your wish will come true."

"Usually I don't want to go to school," Eddie muttered. "But I'd do just about anything to see a Harry Headbanger concert."

"School wouldn't be so bad if it weren't for Mrs. Jeepers," Melody added.

"She's not always mean," Liza said softly. "After all, she did ask Harry Headbanger to play at school tomorrow."

"I wish this snow would melt tonight," Howie said. "Then we wouldn't miss the concert."

"I wish Mrs. Jeepers weren't so mean," Eddie added, "then I wouldn't mind school so much."

None of the kids paid much attention as Eugene began to laugh.

4

Heat Wave

"This is one day I'm glad there was school," Eddie said to his friends as he sank into his seat the next day. "I can't wait for the concert." The morning bell had not yet rung, and Mrs. Jeepers was already writing assignments on the board. There were puddles on the classroom floor, and several buckets sat around the room to catch water from the leaking roof.

Howie nodded and looked out the window. The sun was shining bright, turning yesterday's mountain of snow into ponds of water. "But this crazy weather sure has made a mess. Most of Bailey City is flooded."

"I don't care, I'm just glad the snow

melted," Melody told him. "The concert will be fantastic."

Mrs. Jeepers turned around quickly, causing her purple polka-dotted skirt to swirl. "I am sorry, students. The principal informed me this morning that because of the flood, Harry Headbanger and his band will not be able to perform for us today. Their instruments were damaged from all the water."

"They don't have to play instruments," Melody told her. "They could just sing."

"We'll tap our feet, and Eddie can play his comb," Liza begged.

"That is very thoughtful of you, but the group has already canceled," Mrs. Jeepers explained and continued writing on the board.

"That stupid snow has caused nothing but trouble," Eddie complained.

"You're the one who wished for no school," Melody pointed out.

"Then you wished the snow would

melt," Liza reminded Howie.

"And *it did!*" Howie called out.

"So what?" Eddie muttered. "We're still missing the concert."

"Don't you think it's strange that both of our wishes came true?" Howie asked.

"My wish did, too," Melody pointed out. "I wished for that junkyard to be cleaned up."

"So?" Eddie said softly. "I wished that Mrs. Jeepers would be nice and that hasn't come true. Just look at all the work she's putting on the board."

The four kids looked at their teacher just as she dropped a piece of chalk. "I cannot work in these miserable conditions. Even the chalk is wet. There is no use trying to work today," she told her surprised students. "Let us spend the day watching videos and playing games."

Several students cheered, but Melody gulped and looked at Howie as they remembered Eddie's wish. "Mrs. Jeepers never lets us watch a video," Melody whispered.

"Shall we make it a party?" Mrs. Jeepers continued. "I will have some cookies sent in."

Eddie hollered out, "Can we have ice cream, too?" The rest of the class grew silent. Mrs. Jeepers hated for anyone to yell in her class. But her eyes didn't flash and she didn't rub her brooch. She smiled a big toothy grin instead of her usual odd little half smile.

"Certainly," Mrs. Jeepers said.

"It looks like all our wishes have come true," Howie said when they reached the oak tree after school.

"Wishes just don't come true like that. I've wished for plenty of things and they didn't come true," Eddie argued.

"That's right," Melody agreed. "Nobody can make wishes come true."

"Nobody, except a genie in a magic bottle." Liza giggled.

"That's it!" Howie shouted. "Remember the green bottle we found?"

Liza jumped up and down. "That must have been a genie's bottle, and we let him out. That's why our wishes are coming true!"

"Then where is the genie?" Melody asked.

The four kids heard a bicycle horn as Eugene rode into his backyard and waved. Melody and Howie waved back. But Liza's eyes were big as she pointed.

"There's the genie. You just waved at him."

"Liza, you've popped your cork," Eddie teased. "Genies are only in fairy tales. Besides, they don't ride purple bicycles. They fly on magic carpets."

"Don't be so sure that Liza's crazy," Howie told him. "Remember that Eugene showed up right after we opened the bottle."

"He sure looks like a genie," Melody agreed.

"And his name is EUGENE," Liza said.

Eddie laughed. "The next thing you know, you'll have Arabians on horseback taking over Bailey City. There's no such thing as a genie. After all, if I could do magic, I'd be better-looking than him."

"Shh, he'll hear you," Liza warned Eddie.

"Who cares?" Eddie bellowed. "What's he going to do? Wish me into Aladdin's

lamp? You guys are stupid to believe slush like that."

"I wish you'd shut up," Melody snapped at Eddie. She was about to punch him in the arm when the kids heard booming laughter from the yard next door.

Melody's eyes got big and she whispered, "Oh my gosh, what have I done?"

5
Croak

Eddie trudged across the muddy playground the next morning as his three friends waited under the oak tree.

"I guess we were silly to think Eugene is a genie," Howie said. "Eddie had plenty to say yesterday, even after you made that wish."

"You're right," Melody laughed. "No one can make Eddie shut up."

Eddie stopped in front of his friends and glared at Melody. "What's wrong?" Melody asked.

Eddie opened his mouth to answer. But all that came out was a sickly croak.

"Are you sick?" Liza asked.

"CROAK!" Eddie said again.

Melody's eyes got big. "Oh, no! My wish did come true."

"It's just laryngitis," Howie said.

Eddie nodded. Then he croaked some more. This time his friends could tell what he was saying. "Grandma gave me this terrible medicine. She said I'll be fine in a few days. It has nothing to do with that stupid wish."

"But you can barely talk," Melody pointed out.

Howie nodded and looked at their neighbor's house. Eugene waved to them from his porch. Howie waved back and then whispered to his friends, "The weird weather could have made Eddie lose his voice."

"Or it could have been Melody's wish," Liza interrupted.

"Shhh," Howie warned. "From now on, we need to be very careful not to let Eugene hear us. And no more wishing! Just in case he is a genie."

Eddie shook his head and squeaked, "I can prove he's no genie."

"How?" Melody asked.

"I'll just make a wish," Eddie croaked. "I wish—"

Howie slapped his hand over Eddie's mouth with a loud smack. Eddie tried to get free, but Howie held on tight.

"Maybe Eddie's right for once," Melody said slowly. "The only way to know for sure is to make another wish. But it must be for something unusual so we know it's not just a coincidence."

Howie dropped his hand, and Eddie glared at him. "And something we really want," Eddie squawked.

"I've got it!" Liza yelled before her friends could stop her. "I wish for French fries, pizza, and chocolate candy for lunch every day!"

They looked at Eugene to see if he had heard. Goose bumps ran down their backs as he bowed and then continued polishing his purple bicycle.

6

Junk Food

"That was a stupid wish," Melody snapped as they headed inside the school. "Why didn't you wish for something good?"

"I did!" Liza cried. "Pizza and chocolate are good."

Eddie put his hands on his hips and croaked, "Those cafeteria ladies would never let us have junk food for lunch every day. I'm telling you there is no such thing as genies, especially in Bailey City."

But Eddie was wrong about lunch. As soon as the bell rang, Mrs. Jeepers cleared her throat and said, "There is some bad news. The food delivery truck has broken down. The cafeteria cannot serve the chicken-and-broccoli bake that was on the menu."

"Too bad," Eddie said hoarsely.

"What are we having for lunch today?" Melody asked.

Mrs. Jeepers shook her head. "I am sure the cafeteria workers will come up with something good."

"That would be a real change," muttered Eddie.

By lunchtime, Liza was starved. "I can't wait for the pizza," she told Melody.

"You don't know we're having pizza," Melody said. "We'll probably end up with fish sticks."

Liza shook her head. "All your wishes came true. So will mine."

Everyone at Bailey Elementary was surprised to find the cafeteria serving their favorite foods. Everyone, that is, except Howie, Liza, Melody, and Eddie.

"Having our own personal genie might

not be so bad," Liza giggled as she bit
into a slice of pizza.

"This still doesn't prove anything,"
Eddie croaked, and squirted ketchup on
his French fries. "Delivery trucks can
break down any time. It's not magic."

"Well, I'm glad it did today," Melody
said. Then she took her tray back for a
second helping of everything.

They were stuffed by the time they

finished. "I couldn't eat another bite," Howie moaned.

"I never want to see another chocolate bar in my whole life," Melody added. There were at least fifteen candy wrappers scattered on their table.

Eddie burped. "I feel terrible. I don't even want to go out for recess."

Liza nodded. "We could just rest by the oak tree."

Melody held her stomach and groaned as the kids sprawled under the oak tree at recess. "Maybe having our own genie isn't so great."

"We don't have a genie," Eddie squeaked.

"But my wish came true!" Liza argued. "That proves Eugene is a genie!"

"That doesn't prove anything," Eddie said roughly.

"It *is* hard to explain why the delivery truck broke down on the same day Liza made her wish," Howie said.

"So what?" Eddie said. "After all, my dad's truck hardly ever works."

Howie pointed to a snazzy red sports car as it drove by the playground. "Your dad ought to have that."

"Wow! I wish my dad had that car!" Eddie blurted out.

Before they could bat an eye, the sports car screeched to a stop, and Eddie's father stepped out.

7

Hocus-Pocus

"That's really a neat car your dad has," Howie said the next morning before school. The four friends were gathered under the oak tree on the warm December day.

"I'd love to zip around in that," Melody agreed.

Eddie frowned and muttered, "Dad just got it because he has to go out of town on business."

"But it's almost Christmas," Liza said.

"My dad doesn't give a jingle bell about Christmas," Eddie snapped.

"Maybe if you make a wish the genie will change things," Melody suggested.

Eddie kicked a puddle of mud and splashed the oak tree. "I don't believe in that hocus-pocus. I still say you're crazy."

"You could be wrong," Howie told him. He unzipped his blue bookbag and pulled out a large book. "I went to the public library last night and found this."

"You must be a genius." Eddie slapped his forehead. "You found a book in a library."

Howie ignored Eddie and opened the book. He showed his friends the section called *Genies: A Wish Come True.*

"Look at the picture!" Melody said. The kids looked at a large picture of a genie coming out of a green bottle. The genie looked exactly like Eugene.

No one said anything as Howie read. "'Genies may be held captive in bottles for thousands of years. The legend says that anyone, young or old, who frees a genie from his entrapment in a bottle shall be granted three wishes. The genie is then free from the curse of the bottle

and no more wishes shall be forth-coming.'"

"Fantastic!" Melody yelled. "There's four of us with three wishes each. That's twelve wishes!"

"We could wish for a whole toy store if we want," Liza laughed.

Howie closed the book and put it back in his backpack. "I think we'd better be careful what we wish for."

"I think you all need therapy," Eddie stomped in the mud puddle again.

"It's worth a try," Liza shrugged. She watched as Eugene pedaled into his back-yard. He honked his bicycle horn and waved. As he hopped off his purple bike and leaned it against the back porch, Liza said, "I wish I had a lifetime supply of bubble gum."

"I wish we could stay up all night," Howie said. "And I wish my mom wouldn't fuss at me."

"Is that the best you can do?" Eddie

asked. "Now this is a good wish . . . I wish for a million bucks."

Liza shook her head. "We ought to wish for something to help the world. I wish people would be nice to each other."

The school bell kept them from making any more wishes and from noticing Eugene smiling in their direction.

8

The *Nice* Surprise

"I had a great time," Howie told Eddie as they walked to school the next day.

"You should stay over every night," Eddie agreed.

Melody and Liza walked up behind them. "What are you guys talking about?" Melody asked.

"Howie spent the night with me last night and we played video games until one in the morning," Eddie explained.

Melody looked at Howie. "I can't believe your mom let you sleep over on a school night. She's usually so strict."

Howie nodded. "She was really weird yesterday. She didn't even fuss about my room being a mess."

The four friends reached the steps in

front of Bailey Elementary. Eddie and Howie sat down on the top step.

"My mom was nice yesterday, too," Liza told them. "She took me shopping and bought me five new outfits. The lady in the store was so happy, she gave us an extra dress for free!"

"It must be *Be Nice to Kids Week*," Eddie said. "I thought my dad would bust a gut when I splattered blue paint all over his new red car, but he just shrugged and helped me wipe it off. It was eerie!"

Just then Carey, a girl from their class, stopped at the bottom of the steps. "Did you study for the science test?" she asked. "I studied for three hours!"

Liza's eyes got big. "I forgot all about the test. I was too busy trying on my new clothes."

Melody sighed. "I couldn't study. All this melting snow damaged our roof, and water was dripping everywhere. My science book got soaked."

"We studied," Howie told them.

Eddie nodded. "Right after we finished playing video games."

"Eddie studied?" Melody gasped. "That's a first."

"I bet I get the highest grade in the class," Carey bragged and climbed the steps. Just when she reached the top step, she stumbled and fell backwards. Melody caught her, but Carey's books and papers flew everywhere. Before Carey could mutter a sound, Eddie hopped up and dashed after her homework. He caught all the papers before they blew away.

Eddie handed the papers to Carey. "You have to watch that top step. Are you okay?"

Carey blushed. "I think so. Thanks for picking up my stuff."

"No problem." Eddie shrugged and held the door open until Carey was inside. When he faced his friends, they were

staring at him with their mouths wide open.

"What's wrong with you?" he asked.

Melody slowly shook her head. "Life at Bailey Elementary will never be the same. First Eddie studies for a test, and then he's actually nice to someone."

"To Carey!" Howie added. "I thought you didn't like Carey."

Eddie's face turned as red as his hair. "Just because I was nice doesn't mean I like her," he snapped.

"*Nice!*" Liza shrieked. "Don't you know what's happened? Everyone's being nice!"

Howie patted Liza on the back. "There's nothing wrong with that."

Liza looked at each of her friends. "But people are being too nice. Don't you remember our wishes? I wished for people to be *nice* to each other."

The four kids were quiet as they thought about their wishes from the day before.

Then Eddie said, "People can be nice without a genie's magic."

"Sure they can," Melody agreed. "When our minister was sick, we all took turns bringing him hot meals."

"But what about Eddie's dad and Howie's mom? Isn't it strange for them to suddenly be nice right after I made my wish?" Liza asked.

"My dad's been nice before," Eddie said. "He even took me camping once."

"And my mom isn't *that* bad," Howie added.

Liza put her hands on her hips. "Well, I've never gotten a free dress before and I've never seen Eddie be that nice to anyone!"

"Liza's right," Melody said slowly. "Liza's wish *did* come true, so Eugene must be a genie."

"So what are we going to do about Eugene?" Howie asked as he led his friends into the school.

Melody yawned. "I'm too tired to think about genies. After our roof started leaking last night, I didn't get a wink of sleep."

"We were up late, too," Eddie told her. "You don't hear us complaining."

"I couldn't sleep either," Liza said softly. "None of us slept. It's what Howie wished."

"It really is true," Melody said. "Eugene is a genie!"

"Hogwash," Eddie snapped. "Just because we got to stay up late doesn't mean the new neighbor is a bottled magician. After all, I didn't get my wish for a million bucks, and Liza hasn't gotten her bubble gum."

"Then explain why you were nice to Carey?" Howie demanded.

Eddie didn't get a chance to answer because Mrs. Jeepers interrupted them.

9

A Sticky Situation

Mrs. Jeepers stood in the doorway and smiled a big cheerful smile. "Come in, children."

"That smile gives me the creeps," Melody whispered as they went into the room. "It's not natural."

Liza shrugged. "She has to be nice. It was my wish."

Instead of her usual skirt and blouse, Mrs. Jeepers had on blue jeans, sneakers, and a Santa sweatshirt. Her green brooch was pinned to a Santa's hat. "We had such a wonderful time yesterday with our little party," she said, "I decided I did not want it to end." Mrs. Jeepers pulled a bag of bubble gum from her desk drawer and began passing it around. "Shall we have a bubble blowing contest today?"

All the kids in the third grade cheered except for Howie and Melody. They were stunned. "This proves it," Howie said to Eddie.

Eddie shook his head as most of the class gathered around Mrs. Jeepers for their bubble gum. "What about my million bucks?"

Howie thought for a minute. "You wished for snow, for Mrs. Jeepers to be nice, and for that red sports car for your dad. That's three wishes. That's all you get."

Eddie kicked the chair in front of him. "That's not fair. I need one more wish."

"Then you *do* believe Eugene's a genie," Melody said.

"I believe I can blow the biggest bubble," Eddie snapped and ran up to get his gum.

They blew bubbles all morning. Eddie proved he was the best bubble blower in the third grade. He was so good, even Mrs. Jeepers asked for a demonstration. Eddie chewed a new wad of gum until it was soft. Then he blew and blew and blew until the bubble was as big as a basketball.

"That's incredible," Carey giggled and winked at Eddie.

"Too bad you have to pop it," Howie said.

But Eddie didn't pop it. He took the gum out of his mouth and held it up like a balloon. Unfortunately, it caught some of Liza's hair. Liza jerked away, but not soon enough. Eddie's prizewinning bubble popped right on top of her head.

"Look what you've done!" Liza screamed. She started pulling on the gooey strands, but the gum was stuck. "What am I going to do?"

Mrs. Jeepers stood over Liza and Eddie. The class held their breaths waiting for her eyes to glow and for her brooch to work its magic. Instead, Mrs. Jeepers smiled again. "What an unfortunate accident. We will have to cut the gum from your hair. But do not worry, your hair will grow back."

"Here are some scissors," Melody said.

Eddie grabbed the scissors. "I made the mess, I'll fix it."

"*No!*" Liza screamed. But she was too late. Eddie had already snipped off a hunk of hair.

"Hold still," Eddie told her. "I've almost got it all."

Liza whimpered as another hunk of hair fell into her lap. "I hate you," she screamed at Eddie. Then she threw her chewed wad of bubble gum. She aimed at Eddie. But it landed on the chalkboard beside Mrs. Jeepers instead. The entire class froze, even Liza.

Mrs. Jeepers plucked the gum from the chalkboard and wrapped it in a tissue. Howie gulped, and Melody closed her eyes when Mrs. Jeepers faced Liza.

"You are upset by this sticky situation," Mrs. Jeepers said very softly. "Perhaps some time out in the principal's office will help."

Liza's hands shook, and her face turned milk-white. "B. . .b. . .but I've n. . .n. . . never been sent to the principal's office before."

"Then it's high time you went," Eddie said.

"I believe Eddie is correct," Mrs. Jeepers added.

Melody shook her head. "You agree with Eddie?"

"Certainly," Mrs. Jeepers said. "Liza, please go."

The rest of the class stared as Liza slowly left the room. None of them felt like blowing bubbles anymore.

"Let us take our science test now," Mrs. Jeepers said. "Then we will be able to enjoy the afternoon."

The class groaned as Mrs. Jeepers passed out the papers. Howie yawned. "I wish we'd slept last night, but at least we studied."

Melody yawned, too. "I've never taken a test without studying."

Eddie grinned. "I'm a pro at it."

Howie and Melody put their heads down as Mrs. Jeepers gave out the directions. By the time she was finished, they were fast asleep.

10

Nutty

Howie pushed his tray of pizza and chocolate candy to the center of the lunchroom table. "I can't eat this junk again," he said. "My stomach is still churning from all that gum."

Eddie nodded. "My jaws are too sore to eat."

"I never thought I'd be sick of pizza," Melody admitted.

"I never thought I'd get sent to the principal's office," Liza said with tears in her eyes.

Howie patted her back. "You'll get over it. But what about Melody and me?"

Melody nodded. "This has been a terrible day. We slept straight through the test. And it's all Howie's fault."

"My fault?" Howie exclaimed. "What did I do?"

"You made the wish to stay up all night," Melody reminded him.

Liza held up her hand. "It wasn't Howie's fault, it's Eugene's."

"What did Eugene do?" Eddie asked.

"He made the wishes come true," Liza said.

Melody shook her head. "We made the wishes. It's our fault. Not Eugene's."

"Melody's right," Liza said. "And it's up to us to fix things."

"You're as nutty as peanut butter," Eddie laughed. "There's no way you can fix failing a test. Believe me, I know. We can't fix Liza's hair, either."

They looked at Liza. Short yellow spikes stuck out from the back of her head. "It doesn't look that bad," Melody said softly.

"I'll tell you what's bad," Howie said. "It's this heat wave. The snow is melting off Ruby Mountain. The river is rising and if it's not stopped, Bailey City will be flooded—just in time for Christmas."

"That's awful," Liza groaned. "People will be homeless for the holidays."

Howie nodded his head. "And that's just the beginning . . . there's a severe storm heading our way. That means even more flooding unless we do something about it."

"We should use our leftover wishes to

make things better," Liza suggested.

"Liza's right," Melody said.

"I don't have any wishes left," Eddie reminded them.

"I've used all three of mine, too," Howie said.

Liza nodded her head. "Me, too."

"I've just made two wishes," Melody told them. "One was for Eddie to shut up, which didn't last long enough, and the other was for the yard to be clean."

Howie put his hand on Melody's shoulder. "It's up to you. You're the only one who can save Bailey City from flooding."

"Oh, Melody," Liza whispered, "can you do it?"

Melody swallowed slowly and said, "I'll do it."

11

Don't Blow It!

After school the four kids rushed to the oak tree and looked into the stranger's yard. Christmas lights still blinked on the fence and tree. Mean clouds darkened the sky overhead and thunder rumbled nearby. Howie grabbed Melody's arm. "It's now or never," he told her.

"But it's going to storm. We'll get wet."

"More people will get wet if you don't," Liza told her.

"I think you're all soggy," Eddie said.

Melody took a deep breath. "Howie and Liza are right. We have to keep Bailey City from flooding."

"Be careful what you wish for," Liza whispered to Melody.

"Yeah," Eddie muttered, "don't blow it!"

Melody nodded her head and called out, "Eugene, can we see you for a minute?"

But Eugene didn't open the door. The yard and house were completely still, except for the twinkling lights flapping in the wind. Branches of the oak tree whipped around overhead. A small branch tore loose from the tree and flew into Eugene's yard.

"Come out!" Liza hollered. "We know who you are."

"You've ruined everything," Eddie bellowed.

"Shhh," Melody warned, "you'll make him mad."

"Maybe we should thank him for the wishes," Liza said. "After all, some of them did turn out good."

Howie shook his head. "Not one of them did. We've caused a terrible flood, half the school's sick from eating junk, and Mrs. Jeepers will probably lose her job for being too nice."

"And worst of all, Carey thinks I like her!" Eddie sputtered.

"Everything's a mess," Melody agreed. "And this storm will make it worse."

"Where is that bike-riding wish-giver?" Eddie asked. "He's always here after school."

"I don't think he can hear us over the wind," Liza said.

"Let's scream together," Howie told them.

"Eugene!" the four kids screamed. But the only answer was the whistling of the wind as it grew stronger and stronger.

Liza grabbed the fence when a huge gust of wind sent her scarf sailing into the branches of the oak tree, and paper from Melody's notebook flew in every direction. Howie looked up just in time to see a carpet flying past him. But he blinked, and then it was gone.

"This is crazy," Melody screamed as she crawled after her papers.

"We're going to be blown clear to Ruby Mountain," Liza wailed and squeezed the fence tighter. "This is all Eugene's fault."

Melody grabbed a piece of paper that was flying by and screamed, "I wish everything was back to normal!"

12

Four Genies

It was the next morning and the four kids could see the food delivery men unloading boxes of broccoli and corn dogs from their big white truck. The air was crisp and cool, and a thin layer of frost covered the ground. Under the frost, the kids could see litter scattered across the yard behind the school. The twinkling lights were gone, and so was Eugene.

"I guess things really are back to normal," Melody said.

Eddie nodded. "That windstorm really trashed the place up again."

"I thought we were going to be blown over the rainbow by that wind yesterday," Liza said.

201

"But we did it," Melody told them. "We saved Bailey City."

Howie nodded. "The cool weather has stopped the flood. The snow on Ruby Mountain is frozen again."

Eddie pulled his jacket tighter. "I'm glad my dad's company canceled his trip, even if they did take the sports car back."

Melody looked at the empty house. "I think I'm going to miss Eugene."

Howie agreed. "It's not every day you get to meet a real live genie."

"Even if he wasn't a genie, he sure made this old junky yard sparkle," Liza said.

"Hey, what's this?" Eddie yelled as he reached into the branches for a small brown bottle.

"Don't open it!" his friends screamed.

Eddie shook his head. "It's already open, and there's a note inside." The kids huddled around and read the strange handwriting.

"It's from Eugene," Melody told them. "He's telling us we can make our wishes come true."

"Don't tell me you're turning into a genie!" Eddie slapped his forehead.

"Maybe just a little." Melody smiled. "After school I'm going to get some trash bags and clean up that yard myself."

"Are you crazy?" Eddie asked. "That's too much work."

"I'll help you." Liza smiled. "Maybe I have a little genie in me, too."

"Count me in," Howie told them. "Just don't open any strange-looking bottles."

The girls giggled and said together, "*No way!*" Then Melody, Liza, and Howie looked at Eddie.

"What about you?" Melody asked. "Will you help?"

Eddie bowed low. "Your wish is my command."

Pirates Don't Wear Pink Sunglasses

To
Ruth and Charles Dadey
and
Charlene and Walter Jones

1

Mistletoe

"I can't believe we have to go back there," Melody complained as the school bus went over a bump.

Liza leaned her head out the bus window and moaned, "We'll never make it out of there alive. Mr. Jenkins will get us for sure this time."

The Bailey Elementary kids nodded as they remembered last summer at Camp Lone Wolf. They were sure Mr. Jenkins, their camp counselor, was a werewolf.

"He'll have to deal with me first," Eddie said from the seat behind the two girls. He held up a large clump of mistletoe.

"All right!" Howie slapped his friend Eddie on the back. "That should keep old werewolf-face in check." The kids had read in a book that people during the

Middle Ages used mistletoe to scare away werewolves.

Eddie stuffed the mistletoe into his blue Bailey City gym bag. "I still don't believe Mr. Jenkins is really a werewolf, but just in case. . . ."

"You're ready," Melody finished for him.

The four kids were silent as the bus passed the sign that said *Welcome to Camp Lone Wolf*. Tall weeds clung to the weathered sign. As the bus bumped over the gravel drive, Coach Ellison stood up in the front of the bus and grinned at the Bailey School kids.

"I always look forward to this nature trip," he said, rubbing his hands together. "Especially the boat race on Friday against the Sheldon Sharks."

"I don't know why," Liza mumbled. "Bailey School NEVER wins."

Melody nodded. "All we end up with are mosquito bites."

Every year the kids from Bailey Elementary went on a week-long nature trip. And every year the field trip ended with a rowing competition against the kids from nearby Sheldon City. The Bailey Boaters had never won a single race.

"But this time Coach Ellison says we're going to have a professional instructor," Howie told her.

"If Mr. Jenkins doesn't get us first." Melody shivered as she remembered Mr.

Jenkins' wolf-like howls.

"Maybe Mr. Jenkins won't even be there," Liza said.

"Yeah, maybe he retired to the Old Werewolves' Home," Melody said hopefully.

Eddie shook his curly red head and pointed. "Not a chance. Look!"

As the bus squeaked to a stop, the four kids saw a very hairy Mr. Jenkins standing beside a picnic table. He wore no shoes, a brown Camp Lone Wolf T-shirt, and ragged blue jeans. Around his furry neck were silver dog tags. Beside him stood a stocky man with a long black beard and bright pink sunglasses. The stranger's frizzy black hair was tied back in a ponytail with a purple bandana, and a silver earring dangled from his left ear.

"Oh, no!" Melody gasped. "Now there's two of them!"

Howie gulped. "It's a werewolf convention."

"Everybody off!" Coach Ellison hollered from the front of the bus. "Let's get ready for those Sheldon Sharks!"

Liza followed her friends off the bus. "I just hope we don't get eaten first!"

2

Captain Teach

"Welcome to Camp Lone Wolf, Bailey kids," Mr. Jenkins boomed in a voice loud enough to rattle the bus windows. "I hope you're ready to work those rowing muscles of yours."

"I hope he doesn't make a snack out of my muscles," Melody whispered, but she quickly fell silent when Mr. Jenkins glared at her. His eyes were bloodshot and underlined with dark circles. He looked like he hadn't slept since the last time she'd seen him.

"It's kind of you to give us a discount," Coach Ellison said. "The school couldn't afford to pay full price."

Mr. Jenkins scratched his tangled beard and shrugged. "Business has been slow. At least this way the camp is earning some money. And I was lucky to run into Captain Teach. He's helping out at no cost." Mr. Jenkins nodded to the burly man. "Teach knows all about making a crew shipshape, so you rookies pay attention and you'll win that boat race."

"I'd rather eat hot dogs and ice cream," Eddie laughed. But his smile faded when Mr. Jenkins grinned back, showing all his teeth.

Mr. Jenkins licked his lips. "We'll worry about eating later, after Teach is through with you."

Liza gulped. "I'm already worried."

"They're all yours," Mr. Jenkins told Captain Teach as he stalked into the woods.

Coach Ellison held his hand out to the new instructor. "Hello, I'm Frank Ellison, the Bailey coach." Instead of shaking his hand, Captain Teach spit on the dusty ground and adjusted his pink sunglasses.

Coach Ellison dropped his hand to his side and stammered, "We're honored to have an experienced instructor. Where did you get your experience?"

Captain Teach scowled and spoke with a gruff accent. "Me life has been the sea, and I work where the tide takes me." He winked at Coach Ellison and then turned to the kids clustered by the bus. "Why are you sailors loafing about?" he growled. "Get your gear stowed in the cabins and then hightail it to the docks. We've work to do."

The kids ran into each other as they grabbed their bags and headed for the cabins.

Melody, Liza, and the other girls dumped their bags on the bunks in Cabin Gray Wolf. Dust clouds poofed from the mattresses and made them sneeze. "This place is filthy," Melody snapped. "It looks like no one has been here since we left."

Liza knocked some cobwebs down with a pillow. "You're probably right. Everybody's started going to Camp Soaring Eagle on the other side of Sheldon City."

"Camp Soaring Eagle is fantastic," Carey said. "It's much better than this flea nest. It has horses, motor scooters, and even scuba gear. I went there for two weeks! It was a blast!" Carey's father was the president of the Bailey City bank, and she always got to do whatever she

wanted. Most of the kids thought she was a brat.

"I don't think Camp Lone Wolf can afford that stuff," Liza said.

"It won't be able to afford to stay open if it doesn't do something fast," Carey snapped. "My dad said this place is broke. If they don't make this month's payment, Bailey Bank is going to take over."

"What does a bank want with a camp?" Melody asked.

Carey smiled. "They're going to sell it to Mega-Mall Development Company so Bailey City can have the biggest mall in the country."

"But we already have a mall," Melody reminded Carey.

Liza looked out the dusty window at all of the tall pine trees. "It'd be a shame to tear down all those trees. And what about the animals and Mr. Jenkins?"

Carey shrugged. "Who cares about that

mangy man and all those nasty creatures? A mall would be great!"

"I'm not so sure," Liza muttered as the girls headed back outside.

They met Eddie and Howie outside Cabin Silver Wolf. Tall weeds sprouted around the cabin. "This place is a mess," Howie said.

"It's gone to the dogs," Eddie laughed. "Or should I say the wolves?"

Liza's face turned pale. "Maybe wolves have taken over. After all, I haven't seen any other camp counselors."

"Liza's right," Melody said.

Eddie laughed at his friends. "I have plenty of mistletoe with me. Besides, Coach Ellison and Captain Teach are here. We have nothing to worry about."

Howie took a deep breath and looked at his friend. "I hope you're right."

3

Long-Tongued Jack

Coach Ellison herded the group down to the lake where Captain Teach waited. He stood on two boats, with one foot in each boat.

Melody nodded. "Look at his parrot." Perched on Teach's shoulder was a large yellow-and-green bird with a bright orange beak.

"Morning," the bird chirped.

"Oh, how sweet," Carey said.

"Row, mate!" the bird squawked.

Eddie laughed. "Sweet, just like poison."

"Hardee, har, har," Captain Teach laughed and pushed up his sunglasses. "Long-Tongued Jack here says it be time to get started. We've no time to waste if you're going to win that race."

"But we can't win," Liza whined. "The Sheldon City Sharks always beat the Bailey Boaters."

"Can't never wins! Can't never wins!" Long-Tongued Jack squawked and raised his colorful wings.

"Jack's right," Teach roared. "We'll have no lily-livered quitters here. Captain Teach never gives up without a fight."

"Even if we're the worst rowers in the state?" Eddie asked.

"Especially then," Teach said and adjusted his pink sunglasses. "We'll catch those Sheldon big shots off guard. They'll never know what hit them."

"Now you're talking." Eddie smiled, but the rest of the kids still looked uncertain.

"Surely you pint-sized pieces of fish bait know the story of Molly the Red?" Captain Teach looked at the kids shaking their heads.

"Molly the Red, Molly the Red!" Long-Tongued Jack screeched and flew over to Coach Ellison and sat on his head. A few kids snickered. Coach Ellison stood very still as Teach began telling his story.

"It was back in 1718 when pirates still ruled the seas. Molly the Red was the fiercest pirate ever to sail up the Northern Coast. Most pirates were content to stay near the Barbary Coast where it was safe. But not Molly. She feared not a thing, 'cepting maybe Blackbeard himself."

A few kids nodded their heads in recognition of the name Blackbeard, the most famous pirate who ever lived.

"Molly's ship was loaded with riches she'd looted from ships sailing from the East Coast harbors. She needed a place to hide out for a while to bury her treasures. That place was —"

"Bailey City," Coach Ellison interrupted.

Long-Tongued Jack flapped his wings and squawked, "Bailey Treasure! Bailey Treasure!"

"But Bailey City isn't on the ocean," Howie pointed out.

"Aye. A smart lad you be. The original settlement of Bailey City was right here on the shores of the Red River, which flows into the Atlantic."

"I never knew pirates were in Bailey City," Liza said with wide eyes.

Teach shook his head. "The scallywags never made it. Molly thought that Bailey City would be an easy mark of yellow-bellied men and women, a good place to rob and plunder and hide out. But Bailey City had a surprise for her."

"What happened?" Melody asked.

"When some of the gentle folk of Bailey City heard that Molly's thieving rascals were on their way, they ran off. But some had the guts to stay. They built barricades and practiced with their weapons, women and men alike. They were ready when Molly's ship, heavy with treasure, rounded the bend to Bailey City."

"Did Molly's pirates loot Bailey City?" Howie asked.

"Hardee, har, har," Captain Teach roared. "Hardly! The men and women of Bailey City blew that ship clear out of the water."

"What about the treasure?" Carey asked.

"Never found," Teach whispered. "Some think it's still here, buried by that thieving woman somewhere on the shores of the Red River."

The kids looked at the blue water, wondering about the treasure, until Eddie interrupted. "This is all very interesting," he said to Captain Teach, "but what does it have to do with the race?"

"Everything!" Teach said, slowly adjusting his pink sunglasses. "We're going to do the same thing to the Sheldon Sharks that they did to Molly the Red. We're going to blow them out of the water!"

4

Treasure

"You scallywags look to be getting the hang of it now, I see," Captain Teach bellowed from the dock. "Tomorrow you'll be ready for a real workout!"

"But we are working," Liza said. The entire third grade practiced rowing all afternoon under Captain Teach's strict command. Eddie started off by splashing the kids with his oars. But one "Buckle down, mate," from Captain Teach stopped Eddie's mischief.

"Watch out!" Liza screamed. Just as the four friends were getting the hang of rowing, a speed boat zipped past leaving huge waves in its wake. Eddie and Melody frantically turned the boat away from the rushing water while the waves crashed against their tiny boat. Howie

dropped his oar and Liza screamed.

"Hardee, har, har," Teach roared from the dock. "I see you landlubbers know nothing about water. If you see ripples coming at you, face them head-on. That way the waves will rock you like a baby in a cradle!"

After that, no one goofed off, and everyone improved. The next time a boat sped past, they rode out the waves like experts. "We're getting pretty good at this," Eddie bragged.

Captain Teach threw his head back and laughed. "You city slickers are barely moving the boat. You have a long way to go before you'll beat those Sheldon rogues."

"Sheldon rogues! Sheldon rogues!" Long-Tongued Jack screeched from Teach's shoulder. He flapped his wings when Captain Teach hopped into a boat. Teach showed Howie how to tie the boat to the dock with a tight hitching knot, then he grinned at the tired campers. "You rascals need to eat. You'll need to muster all your strength for tomorrow's workout," he said. "So eat hardy, mates!"

"All right, I'm starving," Liza cheered.

Captain Teach waited until the last boater was safely on the dock before he stomped off toward the cabins. The other boaters ran ahead with Coach Ellison, but Liza was too tired to keep up. Melody, Howie, and Eddie slowed down to walk with her.

"My arms are killing me," Liza said as the kids followed a good distance behind Captain Teach.

Melody nodded her head. "I've never worked so hard in my whole life."

"That Teach is a real battle-ax," Eddie agreed, looking up the trail at Teach's huge back, "but he might just make winners out of us."

"You mean you like him?" Howie asked, rubbing his sore arms.

Eddie shrugged. "I wouldn't exactly say I like him, but I do like to win. Captain Teach sure seems to know about rowing. If we keep this up, those Sheldon Sharks won't stand a chance. I never thought I'd say this, but I'm glad nature week is at Camp Lone Wolf."

"You better enjoy it here while you can," Liza told him. "Carey told us that the camp is probably going to close."

"What are you talking about?" Howie asked.

Melody explained, "The camp is losing money. If Mr. Jenkins can't make this month's payment, the bank is going to turn it into a huge mall."

Liza looked at the tree-lined trail and sighed. "I still think it would be a shame to tear down these huge old trees. I bet some of them were here when Molly the Red terrorized the first Bailey City."

"That's what Camp Lone Wolf needs," Howie told them. "Molly the Red's treasure."

"You're right," Melody agreed. "Captain Teach said it was never found."

"Maybe we could find it!" Liza squealed.

Eddie shook his head. "If it hasn't been found in over two hundred years, there's no way we could find it. We'd better concentrate on beating the Sheldon Sharks."

"I guess you're right," Liza said. "Still, it would be nice to save those big trees."

Eddie bent down to pick up a small green case that was in the middle of the trail. "I think Teach dropped this," he said.

"It's his sunglasses case," Liza said. "We can give it to him in the dining hall."

"It's empty except for a piece of paper,"

230

Eddie told his friends as he unsnapped the case.

"That's none of your business," Liza told him and tried to jerk the case away.

"Liza's right," Howie agreed.

"A little peek won't hurt anything," Eddie muttered. "Besides, we don't even know for sure it's Teach's. I'll see if there's a name inside." Eddie pulled a yellowed piece of paper from the back of the case and carefully unfolded it. Strange lines covered the small paper, and wispy handwriting filled one corner.

"There's a note on it," Eddie said.

Melody snatched the paper from

Eddie. "Reading other people's mail is against the law."

Eddie shrugged. "It's just an old map anyway."

"Why would Teach keep an old map in his sunglasses case?" Liza asked.

"He probably uses it to plan our rowing training," Howie suggested.

"Maybe we should keep it so he won't be able to plan any more killer workouts," Melody said as she folded the map and stuffed it back in the case.

"That wouldn't be honest," Liza told them. "We'll give it to him at dinner."

When they finally reached the dining hall, Coach Ellison was helping Mr. Jenkins grill hamburgers and hot dogs. But Captain Teach was nowhere in sight.

5

Blackbeard

"We have to give his sunglasses case to him," Liza told her friends. "He might be worried about it." The kids had swallowed down their entire supper of hot dogs, hamburgers, French fries, baked beans, and ice cream and still there was no sign of Captain Teach in the dining hall.

"We have plenty of time before the campfire," Melody said.

Eddie frowned and licked the last bit of ice cream off his fingers. "We don't know where Teach is staying."

"Teach is in that small cabin close to the boat dock," Carey said as she walked past their table to put up her food tray. "I saw him going there after he practically killed us this afternoon."

"It's settled then," Liza said, gathering up her tray. "We'll go right now."

"I don't know how I ever got mixed up with a bunch of turkeys like you guys," Eddie complained as they walked down the path to the lake.

"There's the cabin," Howie said. "I never even noticed it before." Howie pointed through the trees at a small cabin set back from the path. The gray wooden cabin had a tiny porch with a flag hanging from it.

"That's a weird flag," Melody said as they walked onto Captain Teach's porch. The flag was black with a white skull painted on it, and crossed bones were underneath the skull.

"That's a Jolly Roger," Howie told them. "Teach must like to study about pirates."

"How do you know that's a pirate flag?" Eddie asked, "For all you know, it could be the flag of Brazil. Maybe Teach is from Brazil."

"If you'd read a book once in a while you'd learn something," Howie said as he knocked on the door.

"He's not here," Eddie said. "Are you happy now? We walked all the way down here for nothing."

"Try one more time," Liza suggested.

Howie knocked on the door again. This time his pounding caused the door to slowly creak open. Howie peeked inside the cabin. He looked back at his friends and gulped. "Captain Teach isn't here, but you'll never believe what is."

Eddie pushed past Howie into the cabin. "Wow, this is neat!" Eddie shouted. The walls of the cabin were covered with swords, old guns, and yellow maps. A large bird perch stood near the window, and a bookcase was crammed full of model ships in glass bottles.

"I've always wanted one of these," Eddie said, picking up a huge ship in a bottle labeled *Queen Anne's Revenge*.

"You'd better put that down before you break it," Liza said. "We can just leave the case on the porch."

"I don't think we'd better leave anything," Howie told them. "I have a strange feeling about all this."

"What are you talking about?" Melody asked.

"Let me see that map again," Howie asked Melody. She shrugged and handed over the green case. Howie carefully unfolded the old map and held it up by the window to read its strange handwriting.

"You shouldn't read that," Liza reminded him.

Howie looked at Liza and spoke very seriously. "This may be a matter of life and death. Besides, this isn't a letter. It's just a note scribbled on a map."

"I guess it's okay. Can you read what it says?" Liza said.

Howie carefully smoothed out the old crinkled paper and tried to make out the words. He read, " 'My dearest Black-beard, I am doomed. I leave you my treasure and my love.' "

Liza squinted to read the strange hand-writing. "Do you think it's from Molly?"

"Molly the Red?" Melody asked.

Howie nodded his head. "And I bet this is a map telling Blackbeard where her treasure is buried."

"You're crazy," Eddie said, grabbing the map back. "What would Teach be doing with a pirate's map?"

"In the same book that had the pirate's flag, there was also a section about Black-beard," Howie told them.

"That makes sense," Melody said. She touched a huge sword that hung from the wall. "After all, Blackbeard was the most famous pirate who ever lived."

"Also the meanest," Eddie agreed.

Howie pointed to the ship in the bottle Eddie had held up. "That was his ship.

Read the name on the bottom of the label."

Eddie held the bottle up to read the label in the fading light. " '*Queen Anne's Revenge.* Ship of Blackbeard, Captain Edward Teach, killed 1718.' "

"Captain Teach!" Melody squealed.

"So what?" Eddie put the bottle back on the shelf. "You said yourself Teach likes to study about pirates. Captain Teach is probably his nickname."

Howie shook his head. "I don't think Teach just likes to study about pirates. I think he *is* a pirate."

Eddie laughed out loud. "Pirates lived a long time ago. There aren't any left today."

"Besides, who ever heard of a pirate wearing pink sunglasses?" Melody said.

"I don't know," Liza said. "Let's just leave the case and go."

"We can't." Howie shook his head. "We know too much. If this is a treasure map and Teach really is a pirate, we may be in a lot of danger."

"Danger. Danger. Squawk!"

The four kids jumped at the loud screech. There, perched on the window-sill, was Long-Tongued Jack.

6

Birdbrain

"Run!" Melody screamed and darted for the door along with her friends. They collided before they could squeeze through, and Liza went sprawling across the floor. Howie tripped over her and landed with a thump.

"Ouch!" Liza cried. "You hurt my leg."

"Peg leg! Peg leg!" Long-Tongued Jack crowed.

"I'd like to give you a peg leg, you birdbrain!" Eddie hissed at the bird.

Long-Tongued Jack flapped across the room and landed right on Eddie's curly red hair. "Squawk! Birdbrain. Birdbrain."

"Cut that out!" Eddie shook his head and Jack flew to his bird perch.

Melody giggled. "It looks like Jack knows who has a birdbrain."

Howie sat up and rubbed his elbow. "Shhh. Teach must be nearby. We have to get out of here, before it's too late."

The four kids peeked out the door. The trail was clear, so they silently slipped out of the cabin. They were sneaking down the trail when a sound from behind a huge oak stopped them dead in their tracks.

"What might you scallywags be up to? You should be down at the campfire," Teach grumbled in his raspy voice.

The four kids turned to face Teach. Howie shoved the green sunglasses case deeper into his pocket, and Liza squeezed behind Eddie and Melody.

"We're just out exploring the woods," Melody stammered.

"Admiring the plants and stuff," Eddie added.

"Hardee, har, har," laughed Teach. "Then you've found my favorite wild-flower in these woods."

Teach pointed to a group of flowers that were nearly as tall as the kids. "See how those bright orange blossoms hang around the stem like a necklace on a lady's neck?" Teach asked. "They shimmer like gold. Aye, these be my favorite flower in the woods. But they have a secret, too."

"What?" Liza asked.

"Come closer," Teach said. "I'll show you."

The four kids inched closer to Teach as he held up a stem with the dangling orange flowers. "Do you see the green jewel? It hangs beneath the blossom." Teach pointed to a small seed pod. "Go ahead. Touch it."

When Liza reached out and tapped the pod, seeds exploded against her nose.

"Wow! That's neat," Eddie laughed and reached over to tap a few seed pods himself. "An atom bomb flower!"

"What's it called?" Howie asked.

"Some call it jewel-weed," Teach said with a smile. "But others have another name for it. The same thing that Molly the Red said about her very own treasure of riches."

"What?" the four campers asked.

"Touch-me-not!" Teach said. Then he squeezed a dangling pod and sent a seed pinging against Eddie's forehead.

"Squawk! Touch-me-not! Touch-me-not!" Long-Tongued Jack called from the nearby tree.

Teach winked at the campers before him. "Aye, tis best not to touch the jewels of pirates. But the jewel-weed is a jewel of nature, here for us all to enjoy." Then Teach began to laugh. Only this time, his laughter sent cold chills racing up the four kids' backs.

"We'd better get back to camp," Melody said as she backed away from Teach.

"Aye," Teach nodded. "Ye best be trotting back to the others before they think something bad has befallen you."

The four friends left Teach standing next to the clump of jewel-weed and hurried to the campfire. All the other kids were roasting marshmallows and listening to Coach Ellison talk about wildflowers. Howie, Melody, Liza, and Eddie huddled near a huge maple tree.

"Now do you believe Teach is a pirate?" Melody asked Eddie.

Howie nodded. "He's here at Camp Lone Wolf to find Molly the Red's treasure."

"And he knows we have the map. That's why he was warning us against touching the treasure!" Liza whimpered.

Eddie shrugged. "Teach is here to help us win that race against Sheldon. And the only treasure around here is buried in a box of Cracker Jack. He was just showing us a flower in the woods."

Howie shook his head. "I'm not so sure. If the legend about Molly the Red is true, then her treasure is buried on the shores of Red River here at Camp Lone Wolf."

Eddie pointed to the run-down cabins. "If there was a treasure here, Mr. Jenkins would have castles instead of those rat traps."

"Exactly!" Liza blurted. "If we could find that treasure, we could help Mr.

Jenkins save the camp . . . and all these huge old trees."

"There is no treasure," Eddie told her. "And I can prove it."

"How?" Melody asked.

Eddie held out his hand. "Give me the case. I'll prove that Teach is just a boat instructor because I'll prove there's no treasure."

"How can *you* find it if Teach can't?" Howie asked, handing the case to Eddie.

Eddie stuffed the case and map into his back pocket. "Captain Teach doesn't know this place like we do. Besides, he couldn't find it because there isn't a treasure."

"What if Teach figures out you have the map?" Liza asked. "You could be in great danger."

"He won't find out," Eddie bragged. Then he glared at each of his friends.

"Not unless you tell him."

"We won't tell!" they all said together. But none of them noticed the brightly colored bird perched in the tree above them.

7

Molly's Map

"Come on over, kids," Coach Ellison called Melody, Liza, Eddie, and Howie to the campfire. He handed each one a stick with a marshmallow on one end. "There's nothing like marshmallows roasted over an open fire," he told them.

"Unless it's a roasted scoundrel," Captain Teach bellowed as he came up the path.

Eddie gulped and pushed the eyeglasses case deeper into his back pocket before holding his marshmallow above the roaring campfire.

"Nice job this afternoon." Coach Ellison nodded to Teach. "I've never seen a Bailey team row better."

"Tomorrow, we'll see how they fare rowing at a racing speed," Teach said.

"Are you sure their muscles are ready for that?" Coach Ellison asked.

Before Teach could answer, Long-Tongued Jack swooped down from a treetop and flapped around Eddie's head. "Birdbrain! Birdbrain!" he squawked.

"Cut it out!" Eddie yelled and threw a marshmallow at the bird.

All the kids around the campfire laughed. "I think Long-Tongued Jack likes you," Carey teased.

"I'll make that bird into a feather duster if he doesn't leave me alone." Eddie ducked when Long-Tongued Jack soared around him again.

"Molly's Map!" Long-Tongued Jack fluttered over Eddie's head. "Birdbrain! Molly's Map!"

Coach Ellison looked at Teach. "Maybe you'd better call your bird away before someone gets hurt."

Teach looked at Eddie and rubbed his

beard. "Long-Tongued Jack, quit your flapping."

Long-Tongued Jack swooped over Eddie's head and settled on Captain Teach's left shoulder. Teach reached up and gently smoothed Jack's feathers. "There, there. No use getting ruffled on a night as perfect as this."

"Perfect for what?" Carey called out.

Captain Teach held up a telescope and grinned. "The skies are clear and there'll be a full moon this evening. Tis perfect for spying on the stars!"

The campers leaned back and stared into the night sky as Captain Teach pointed to the twinkling dots of light in the darkening sky. "See them shimmer?" he asked. "They sparkle like diamonds in a treasure chest."

"Did you hear that?" Melody hissed.

"Shhh," Howie warned.

"I've spent many a night looking at the sky to help me find my way," Teach continued. Aye, to think that Molly the Red herself gazed upon these very stars!"

"How do you know so much about the sky?" Carey asked.

"Hardee, har, har," Teach laughed. "The stars and the seas are a sailor's friends." He turned and looked straight at Eddie, Melody, Liza, and Howie. His next words made them huddle closer together.

"Haven't you ever heard the old saying? 'Red skies at night, sailors delight. Red skies at morning, sailors take warning.' "

"Squawk!" Long-Tongued Jack added. "Take warning! Take warning!"

8

Sleep

"Did you see the way Teach looked at us?" Melody whispered to Eddie as they walked toward their cabins. It was late, and the tall trees were swaying in the night breeze.

"What do you mean?" Eddie asked.

"Teach knows we have the map," Liza said.

"Shhhh," Eddie sputtered. "Why don't you just announce it to the whole world."

"Long-Tongued Jack already did," Howie said.

"You guys worry too much," Eddie told them. "Tomorrow morning before breakfast we'll have a look around. Then we'll know for sure there isn't any treasure."

"See you tomorrow," Melody said as she and Liza went into the girls' cabin.

Inside the boys' cabin, Eddie tossed and turned all night long. Once, he was sure he heard a wolf howling. Finally, when the first speck of sunlight popped through the dusty window, Eddie slugged Howie in the arm. "Get up," he whispered.

"Leave me alone," Howie mumbled. "It's still dark."

"The sun is shining. Do you want to waste all day sleeping? I thought you wanted to find out about the pirates' treasure."

Howie moaned and pulled the covers over his head. Eddie shook Howie and then looked out the window. In the early morning light he saw a figure moving toward their cabin. The figure had a bird on his shoulder.

"Howie, let's go! Teach is coming for us!" Eddie threw the blankets off his friend.

Howie took a quick peek out the window and gulped. "What do we do?"

"Hurry, grab your clothes! Let's try the back window!" Eddie ran to the back of the cabin and threw open the squeaky window. Sleepy kids from around the room complained about the noise and snuggled deeper into their covers. None of them noticed as Eddie and Howie slipped out the window.

The boys tiptoed away from their cabin and stopped behind the girls' cabin. Then Eddie felt a cold hand on his shoulder.

Eddie tackled the person behind him. It wasn't until they were both on the ground that he noticed the jet-black pig-tails.

"Ouch!" Melody hissed. "I think you bruised my arm."

Eddie jumped up and brushed off the seat of his pants. "What are you doing here?" he whispered to Melody.

Melody glared up at Eddie. "We saw Teach heading for the boys' cabin and

thought you might need help. What are you doing here?"

Liza giggled from the shadows of a large hemlock tree. "It looked like they were peeking in the girls' cabin."

Eddie's face turned red. "We were not! We were hiding from Teach."

Howie helped Melody up. "Eddie's right. We'd better get out of here before Teach finds us."

"I'm not scared of that mangy sea mongrel," Eddie snapped.

"You sure sounded scared when you saw him coming to the cabin," Howie said.

"And you jumped like a fish out of water when I touched you," Melody added.

"I don't like surprises," Eddie said. "Except for the kind in a treasure chest. That's what I'm going to hunt for." Eddie marched down the trail leading to the Red River. He didn't bother to look behind him. He knew his three friends would follow.

Eddie stopped on the banks of the river and pulled out the sunglasses case. He was smoothing the wrinkles from the old map when Melody, Liza, and Howie stopped beside him.

"I don't think we were followed," Howie whispered.

Liza shivered. "Teach could come after us at any minute."

Eddie laughed. "He won't have a chance. Coach Ellison will see to it that Teach is rowing down the river with the rest of the kids. That gives us plenty of time to look for this make-believe treasure."

Melody pointed to the map. "It'll be impossible to find the treasure. There's no X to mark the spot."

The treasure hunters silently examined the map for several minutes. Then Liza sighed. "Molly the Red must have liked these beautiful trees, too. She even drew some on her map."

"Only those droopy trees on that little island," Eddie pointed out.

Howie snapped his fingers. "Maybe Molly didn't use an X to show where she hid the treasure."

Eddie rolled his eyes. "All professional pirates used an X."

"Not unless they drew trees instead," Melody said slowly and pointed. "One tree has something written on it."

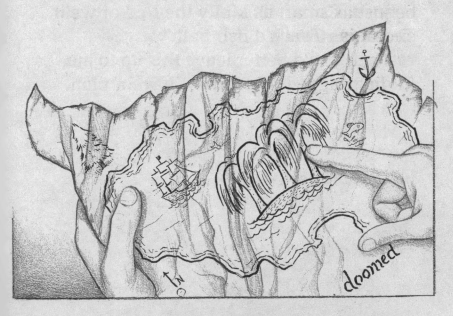

Liza's eyes got big. "Do you mean Molly buried her treasure under those trees?"

"Exactly," Howie told them.

"What kind of pirate makes their map so hard to figure out?" Eddie snapped.

"A smart one," Melody said.

"Wait, I hear Coach Ellison calling us for breakfast," Howie said.

Liza shivered. "We'd better get back. I don't want Teach to come looking for us."

Howie nodded. "And now we have to be just as smart as Molly the Red or we'll end up as Teach's fish bait."

"Then you'd better leave this up to me," Eddie bragged. "Because I have a plan."

9

Soggy Sneakers

Captain Teach and Coach Ellison kept the kids so busy, Eddie didn't have a chance to put his plan into action. Every morning for three days, the kids practiced rowing. In the afternoon, Coach Ellison took them on a hike, and then in the evening they'd practice rowing again or have a nature lesson. On the fourth day, Eddie decided it was time to try his plan.

Eddie, Melody, Liza, and Howie hid under the dock until all their friends had rowed away from shore. Captain Teach stood on the dock, shouting directions. "Heave to, Bailey Boaters! You'll be needing your muscles today. Faster! Faster!"

Long-Tongued Jack flew from a nearby tree and perched on Teach's shoulder.

Teach straightened the pink sunglasses on his nose and looked into the shadows of the dock. The four hiding kids shrunk further into the shadows. Finally, Teach reached up, smoothed Jack's feathers, and whispered something to the bird. Jack flapped his wings and disappeared into the trees behind the four hiding treasure hunters.

"Can we get out now?" Liza whimpered. "I'm soaking wet."

"We all are," Eddie snapped. "We've been sitting in water for an hour."

Melody patted Liza's shoulder. "Don't be so mean, Eddie. I'm beginning to think your plan is as wet as my sneakers."

"They're out of sight," Howie interrupted. "Let's go."

The kids climbed onto the dock and squeezed water out of their clothes. Eddie left a trail of wet splotches as he jogged to a boat.

"Are you sure this is a good idea?" Melody asked.

"You want to get to that island and look for the treasure, don't you?" Eddie asked.

"But what if we capsize the boat?" Liza cried. "We'll drown!"

Howie shook his head. "We won't as long as we remember everything Teach told us about rowing and we wear life jackets. Besides, Eddie's right. This is our only chance."

"While Teach is busy with the other kids," Melody agreed.

Carefully, the four friends climbed in the boat and strapped on the faded orange life jackets. Howie untied the thick knot that held the boat to the dock, and they each grabbed a set of oars. Without a word they dipped them into the water. The boat silently slid away from the dock.

They were halfway to the small island

when a shadow drifted over the boat. Eddie looked up just in time to see the green feathers diving for his head.

"It's that bird!" he screamed and swatted at Jack with an oar, splashing water all over everyone.

"Stop that!" Liza yelled. "You're getting me wet again."

"Tell that bird to stop," Eddie told her.

Long-Tongued Jack landed on Eddie's head. "Birdbrain! Birdbrain!"

"I'm going to pluck that bird bald!" Eddie slapped at the bird, but Jack flapped away and Eddie ended up hitting himself on the head.

"I hope you knocked some sense into yourself," Melody giggled.

"It's not funny!" Eddie snapped. "But at least I scared that bag of feathers away."

Liza nodded as they reached the shores of the little island. "Maybe he'll leave us alone now."

"These trees aren't little like the ones

on the map," Eddie complained, looking up at the huge towering willows as they pulled the boat onto the island.

"Of course not," Melody told him. "Molly the Red made that map over two hundred years ago. The trees were bound to grow a little since then."

"Look for a tree with something written on it," Liza suggested, "like on the map."

"This is a wild goose chase," Eddie muttered. "Blackbeard probably found the treasure and spent it a long time ago."

"I don't think so," Howie said. "Teach said that Molly's ship sank in 1718. That's the same year Blackbeard died. I bet Molly didn't even know he was dead when she wrote the note."

"Oh, how sad," Liza said.

"But it means the treasure is still here," Melody reminded them. "So start looking."

Eddie held up the map and pointed.

"The tree should be over there if this map isn't a fake."

The kids studied every tree, looking for some clue. All they found was smooth bark and lots of mosquitoes. "I feel like a beaver who can't make up his mind," Eddie complained.

"It's hopeless," Liza agreed, looking at the dozens of trees ahead of them.

"I think this is it!" Melody called. "It looks like something is carved on this tree trunk." Her friends ran over to see.

"Oh, my gosh," Liza yelled. "Molly was really here. This is where she left her treasure!"

Just then a willow tree exploded in a flurry of leaves as Mr. Jenkins pushed through the branches. His beard was full of twigs and leaves, and he looked at them with his red eyes.

"There you are!" Mr. Jenkins growled. "I've been following your trail all morning. Why didn't you stay with the others?"

"We just wanted to see what this island was like," Eddie told him.

Mr. Jenkins looked around and spotted the carvings on the willow tree. He traced over them with his huge hairy hand.

"We didn't do that," Liza blurted. "Honest!"

Mr. Jenkins nodded. "The trees here depend on campers not to carve up their barks. And the rest of the Bailey kids were depending on you to help them in tomorrow's race. They're out there practicing right now! I'd better see you rowing like you've never rowed before!"

The four friends scrambled down the path and leaped into their boat. They were in such a hurry, none of them noticed a big bird flapping down the river toward a distant boat.

10

Sailor Take Warning

"If I learn anything else about trees, I'll sprout roots," Eddie complained. Coach Ellison had just given them a nature lesson on chlorophyll, the green stuff in plants. They were sitting around the campfire after rowing practice.

"I think it's interesting," Howie said. "I like learning about nature."

Eddie shook his head. "I might have known you'd be a green freak. Who needs plants, anyway?"

"You do, nickle brains," Liza told him. "Everything on Earth depends on green plants in some way or another."

"I need green plants like a fly needs bug spray," Eddie told her.

Melody rubbed her arms. "I'm so tired

from rowing, my arms feel like limp tree limbs."

"Like those weeping willow tree branches where the treasure is buried," Liza nodded.

"Yeah, I could use some of that chlorophyll myself," Melody laughed.

"Would you guys stop complaining?" Howie said. "I want to know what we're going to do about the treasure."

"We're going to get it," Eddie said.

Liza stood up and dusted off her shorts. "Don't you remember Teach's warning?" she said.

"I'm not worried about that old hair ball," Eddie bragged. "We'll meet first thing tomorrow and dig up the treasure."

The next morning the kids met behind Cabin Gray Wolf. The sun was just coming up, and the sky was blood-red.

"We'd better not go," Liza whimpered. "Look at that sky."

Howie nodded his head. " 'Red skies at morning, sailors take warning.' "

"We're not sailors," Eddie told them. "We're just kids. But, soon, we're going to be rich like pirates!"

"But we'll miss the race against the Sheldon Sharks," Melody said. "Mr. Jenkins said the team was depending on us."

"What's more important?" Eddie snapped. "A flimsy blue ribbon or a chest full of gold?"

Liza, Melody, and Howie nodded their heads. The four kids silently walked down the trail to the dock. With their life jackets on, they paddled out to the island.

"The treasure's this way," Eddie pointed as they pulled the boat onto shore. He led the way through the trees.

"I bet it's a huge chest filled with diamonds and rubies," Melody giggled.

The four kids stopped in front of the carved tree. "This is it," Howie said.

"It *was* it," Eddie gulped. In front of the tree was a big empty hole.

Melody dropped to her knees and checked the ground. "It's gone all right, but check out these paw prints."

"They look like dog tracks to me," Howie said.

"Or wolf tracks," Liza said. "Don't forget Mr. Jenkins saw us here yesterday."

"That stinky werewolf stole our gold!" Eddie yelled, but he got deathly quiet when he was interrupted by the sharp squawk of a parrot overhead.

11

Dead Heat

"What do you think you're doing?" a deep voice growled from behind them. Liza, Melody, Eddie, and Howie turned around to see Captain Teach waving a stick like a sword. "I knew you were up to no good when I saw you sneaking away from camp."

"Squawk! No good. No good," Long-Tongued Jack added from the drooping branches of a willow tree.

"Your mates were depending on you," Teach said.

The four kids backed against the tree trunk when Teach pointed a dirty finger at Eddie. "What's in your hand?"

Eddie looked down at the crinkled treasure map. He quickly wadded it into a tight ball and tossed it into the hole.

"Nothing," he lied. "Just a piece of paper."

"You scoundrels," Teach growled. Then he lunged forward.

"Run!" Howie screamed.

Long-Tongued Jack swooped down out of the tree and followed the kids as they raced to their boat. "Birdbrain!" he squawked.

"Row like you've never rowed before!" Eddie screamed. They jumped in their boat and paddled like the island was on fire. Not far behind was Teach.

"We'll be okay if we can make it back to Coach Ellison and Mr. Jenkins," Howie yelled as he rowed.

"Great!" Eddie hollered. "Our lives depend on a skinny coach and a werewolf!"

"Be quiet and row!" Melody ordered. The kids concentrated on slapping their oars in the water, but they could still hear Teach gaining on them. In the distance, they saw teams of Bailey Boaters and

Sheldon Sharks gliding through the water.

"Faster, faster!" Howie screamed. The kids rowed with all their might. *Slap, slap.* Their boat pulled away from Teach's. *Slap, slap.* With their muscles aching, they could see the dock at Camp Lone Wolf getting closer and closer.

"I don't think I can make it," Liza cried.

"Don't stop now!" Eddie screamed. "We're almost there!"

Liza, Melody, Howie, and Eddie pulled their oars through the water so fast that they soon passed the other Bailey Boaters and the Sheldon Sharks. Ten strokes later they banged against the dock.

Coach Ellison grabbed their boat and helped them out. "That was the best row-

ing I've ever seen," he congratulated them.

The kids were so out of breath, all they could do was point to Captain Teach in his boat. Coach Ellison nodded his head and grinned. "That Teach is a fantastic rowing instructor."

Then he handed the four boaters blue ribbons. "Let's hear it for the new champions of the annual rowing competition."

The four kids barely heard the cheering crowd. They were too busy staring into the wild eyes of Captain Teach.

12

Progress

Captain Teach took two steps toward the foursome before a group of men and women in business suits pushed him aside. "The race is a fitting end to Camp Lone Wolf," one of the women said as the others nodded.

"What do you mean?" Coach Ellison asked.

"Camp Lone Wolf hasn't paid the bank a red cent for months," a man in a blue suit told him. "We're here to take over this property. This will soon be the site of the biggest mall in the country!"

"But what about the huge old trees?" Howie interrupted.

"And all the wildflowers, like jewel-weed and mistletoe!" Liza added. "You can't tear all this down for a mall."

"That's progress," a man in a plaid suit smiled.

"Not to me." The crowd gasped as Mr. Jenkins stepped from the shadows of the forest. His hair was a tangled mess, and deep circles underlined his bloodshot eyes.

"What happened to you?" Coach Ellison asked.

Mr. Jenkins smiled at the crowd. Then his eyes rested on Howie, Melody, Liza, and Eddie. "I've been digging up the money I need to save this place. It looks like the Mega-Mall Development Company will have to look for another place to build."

He faced the men and women in suits. "I treasure this land. Every tree, flower, and animal will always have a home here. Follow me, and we will take care of this matter."

"Wait!" Captain Teach yelled. But as the bankers followed Mr. Jenkins off the

crowded dock, a man in a pinstriped suit accidentally brushed against Teach, pushing him off the dock with a giant splash.

"Squawk! Birdbrain! Birdbrain!" Jack flapped over and landed on Teach's head. Water dripped off his hair, and his glasses hung on one ear.

"I guess we were silly to be afraid of him," Melody laughed, pointing at Captain Teach.

"I wasn't afraid of him," Eddie said, proudly holding his blue ribbon.

"He doesn't look like a pirate, now," Howie said.

"After all," Liza giggled, "who ever heard of a pirate wearing pink sunglasses?"